TALES OF MUNDANE MAGIC

Volume Two

Shaina Krevat

TALES OF MUNDANE MAGIC
Volume Two

A Shaina Krevat book

ISBN: 978-1-7325013-1-7

P.O. Box 5901, Santa Monica, CA 90409

talesofmundanemagic.com

Cover illustration by Igor Canova.

PRINTED IN THE UNITED STATES OF AMERICA

To my amazing sister,
though I am a writer, words fail me on how to
describe how awesome you are

Table of Contents

Gertie and Bridget and Ziggy go shopping

"Bridget? Are you home?"

The door opened, interrupting Gertie's pounding, but instead of her sister it was her roommate Patricia who answered, looking mad enough to call the residential advisor.

"She's out," she said, her words clipped.

"Sorry." Gertie backed away.

"Gertie?"

Gertie turned to see Bridget at the other end of the hall. Ziggy, their ghost dog, barked and ran from her heels to Gertie.

"Ziggy!" Gertie cried, grinning as the dog whooshed up to her face and lapped at her chin. Her baseball cap, firmly on her head and supporting the Wespire Leopards, was enchanted and allowed her to see the ghost of their dead dog. Being licked by a ghost was a cold and unpleasant sensation, but it made Ziggy so happy and it was comforting to have the same relationship in death as they had in life.

"Gertie, what are you doing here?" Bridget asked.

"Demetrius has a new hat and I want to take a look!" Gertie passed her phone to Bridget and patted Ziggy as best she could until he calmed down. A green text message from the manager of the Enchanted Hats Emporium glowed from the screen.

"Can you afford it?" Bridget asked, seeing the price.

"I have enough from tutoring the kids in my potions class." Gertie grinned.

Bridget walked her sister back to her room, where she dropped off her backpack with an apologetic smile at Patricia. Patricia just sniffed in annoyance at Gertie's intrusion and turned away. She and their other roommate's attitudes towards the Mallons and their magic was exactly why Bridget spent so much time in Gertie's private room.

"Can we please hurry?" Gertie asked, nearly shaking in excitement. "You're not going to believe this hat. If it does what Demetrius says it's supposed to do it's going to be awesome!"

The two humans and one ghost made their way to the subway station across the street from Flories Boarding School, descending into the hot halls of the Wespire subterranean transportation system.

The metal train whirred to a stop and the doors opened. Those on the platform waited patiently as a few passengers disembarked. As soon as they were off, the train whistle blew. The ward that kept people from entering dropped, and everyone rushed into the subway at once.

Shoulder to shoulder with other students, Gertie and Bridget shared silent conversations in eyebrow wiggles and pointing with eyes about the lack of personal space from a boy behind Bridget, and the body odor of a jogger who had caught the train at the last minute, still breathing hard and sweating profusely farther down the car.

They got off at thirty-fourth street, along with a couple of other passengers. There wasn't much to interest anyone on the intersection of thirty-fourth and Puckle Place, at least not on ground level.

One of the strangers hit the up elevator button and they all waited. With a *ding*, the elevator doors cranked open.

The four shuffled in. Gertie pushed the "S" button at the top of the column of three buttons. One of the strangers hit the "2" and the doors slid closed.

Another *ding*, and the doors opened on the street level. The stranger that selected the "2" button left, pushing through the "exit" turnstile. Bridget wrinkled her nose as she smelled the stenches of the city kicked up by the pouring rain, and Gertie bit her lip at the sound of the storm.

Ziggy, however, started to wag his tail in excitement.

The doors slid closed and the elevator started dinging, a three note arpeggio of demand. A panel in the elevator wall next to the buttons slid open, revealing what looked like an opal touchpad.

Bridget was the first to pull her card from her pocket and hold it up to the touchpad. Against their father's wishes, Gertie and Bridget's mother had gotten them passports for the magical community. The air between Bridget's card and the touchpad glowed, and the dings stopped, then restarted, bouncing between two notes.

The remaining stranger held her wallet up to the touchpad with her card safely inside. The dings dropped to just one tone.

Bridget released a breath. Since only those who were a part of the magical community were allowed to the top floor of this elevator (for the safety of the community), sometimes people tried to sneak up. Occasionally, just to catch glimpses of the mystical city, but there was always the risk of more sinister reasons. They would claim to have forgotten their passports and try to get the rest of the passengers in the elevator to help them out. There were security measures in place, but it was nice to not have to call on the enchantments that would forcibly remove anyone without a passport.

Gertie finally found her card tucked into the lining of her phone case and held it up. The dinging stopped.

The elevator hummed for a moment, and then started to soar skyward.

The wall behind them dropped, revealing a window for the passengers to watch the ascent. The stranger ignored the view, opting to scroll through emails on her phone, but Gertie and Bridget watched the journey with rapt attention.

The raindrops smacked against the elevator as it flew, creating an intense window-raindrop-race. The girls looked down at the heads of those unaware of the elevator - of the whole city - just above the clouds.

It was a long trip. Magic may be able to distort some things, but physics like g-force would take far too much power to overcome so often. So bubbly music chirped in the background as they waited.

The ghost of Ziggy, invisible to the stranger, sniffed at her shoes, wagged his tail, and enjoyed the view.

Finally, the elevator slowed and there was one last *ding*.

The doors opened and the three stepped into the center of Shipwreck Park. A fountain with statues of magicians in top hats with canes, fairies floating on waves, cats, and an array of other mystical beings stood just in front of them, with a row of trees and other carefully cultivated plants on either side. The cityscape beyond was towering, sparkling from enchantments in the sun, free from the rain below.

The stranger that had accompanied the girls in the elevator removed her long jacket, revealing two black scaly wings and a tail. She stretched and took a few steps, then flapped off into the sky, jacket and briefcase in hand.

They were back in Skyline.

Ziggy yipped and flew around the park in circles.

"Come on, come on, come on!" Gertie shouted, grabbing her sister's arm to drag her.

They walked around the elevator which was embedded in the front half of an old pirate ship lodged in the center of the park. Kids still hunted around in it for secret cupboards full of gold and jewels or treasure maps. Even adults did, sometimes. The sails flapped lazily in the breeze. Gertie, Bridget and Ziggy walked through the park like a little parade, headed for Demetrius' Enchanted Hat Emporium.

It took some walking, a bus, and more walking, but they

managed to make it past the city-famous candy parlor without stopping and to the Emporium.

The Enchanted Hat Emporium was an older building when compared to the rest of its city block. Its brick walls had ivy climbing the sides, creating natural curtains to the high windows that flanked the single wooden door. A neon sign declaring the name of the store and its year of establishment was the only external sign of modernization.

Gertie burst in, sending the bell on the door pealing. A stuffed raven sitting in an open cage by the door shook itself to life, and flew out of the cage, cawing as it fetched someone to help the new customers. Ziggy barked in delight and zipped away after it. Raven and ghost dog swooped up to the second level of the Emporium, a ring with an open center that left the shelves visible from below.

"Thank you, Alice," a voice said, the enchanted animal's keywords to return to its cage. The raven flapped back, slipped inside its cage and froze again. Ziggy, however, could still be heard barking in the back of the shop.

A lanky man appeared at the railing of the second story and groaned. "What are you doing here?"

"I want the fez!" Gertie called back, holding up her phone.

"Oh, is that all?" He slid down one of the ladders and landed with a thump. Demetrius, co-owner and manager of the emporium, pulled at the bottom of his pinstriped vest and made his way to the door. "And I suppose you would like a discount?"

"Well of course I would *like* one," Gertie said with a grin. "A family and friends discount maybe?"

13

"But you're neither friend nor family." Demetrius went behind the checkout desk and pulled out a small blue hatbox.

"Aw, D," Gertie said, leaning against the desk dramatically. "You wound me."

Bridget smiled, already familiar with the strange way that Demetrius and Gertie interacted.

"Good." Demetrius opened the box. "A loyalty rewards discount will be applied."

Gertie's smile stretched like a cheshire cat's from ear to ear. She pulled off her baseball cap and handed it to Bridget, who placed it on her own head. Gertie reached into the box and pulled out a red fez with a black tassel. She placed it on the top of her head and pulled her hands away, waiting for something to happen.

Gertie frowned and glared over at Demetrius.

"Pull the tassel to activate it," he said. "But take a big step to your right."

Gertie opened her mouth to ask why, and suddenly a bright blue light flashed and another Gertie appeared, a big step to her right.

"Woah," Gertie - the old Gertie - said, dropping her jaw.

"Yeah, I know," the new Gertie - the one who had just traveled back in time via the powers of the fez - said. "Now trade spaces with me." She put her hands on old Gertie's shoulders, and the two turned until old Gertie was standing where new Gertie had appeared.

"Now one sharp tug," new Gertie said. Old Gertie reached up and tugged the tassel.

The light flashed again and she was gone.

"So," new Gertie, who at this point was the *only* Gertie, said to Demetrius, "Ten seconds back in time?"

"Twelve, according to the label," Demetrius shrugged. "A bit longer cooldown though. There's never going to be three of you."

"Aw, how terrible," Bridget said, smiling despite her sarcasm. "Why only twelve?"

Gertie looked at her sister incredulously. "Do you have any idea how much power a time travel spell takes?"

"Fair enough," Bridget accepted with a shrug.

"Here's the one manufacturer's warning type of thing, though." Demetrius leaned forward onto the desk. "The spell has, among other protections, a paradox breaker."

"What does that mean?" Gertie asked.

"If you have a future self come back in time, twelve seconds later your hat will make you travel back in time, regardless of whether or not you pull the tassel."

"Great!" Gertie gave two thumbs up.

"But, if it does that, it can damage the hat. If that happens too many times, all you'll have is a fez. No time travel."

"I'll be sure to pull the tassel then." Gertie said, reaching for her wallet. "I need this hat."

"Really?" Bridget asked. "It's only twelve seconds. How much of a difference can that make?"

Demetrius reached swiftly across the desk to slap Bridget across the face. The light flashed and another new Gertie landed next to the desk and grabbed his hand, preventing her sister from getting hit.

"Demetrius!" Old Gertie shouted.

"Gertie!" Bridget said, gesturing. "Go!"

"Oh!" Old Gertie jumped toward the new one and pulled the tassel. She vanished mid-leap, traveling back in time.

"I see your point," Bridget said wryly.

Demetrius pried Gertie's fingers from his wrist.

"I knew you'd stop me," he told her matter-of-factly.

"But in some timelines you slapped her?" Gertie asked, glaring.

Demetrius shrugged. "Depends on your point of view. I like to think the other timelines no longer exist."

Bridget put a calming hand on her sister's shoulder. "Let's take a look around and you can check your bank account to see if you can actually buy it."

Gertie nodded, reluctantly handing the fez back to Demetrius and taking back her baseball cap from Bridget. Bridget guided her sister out of earshot of Demetrius, losing themselves in the shelves of the Emporium.

They saw many unique hats - some in half open boxes and some in glass cases - and even more hats on display with stacks of the same boxes lined in shelves beneath them.

There were top hats - magicians' favorites and able to hold multiple enchantments - cowboy hats - good for animal spells - fedoras, bowlers, deerstalkers, sailor hats, turbans, crowns, veils (wedding and otherwise), spectator hats, smoking caps, bicornes, tricornes, and more. Gertie admired them all and could go on for hours about the pros and cons of different enchantments on different hats, as well as other points of interest like style and history.

"I like the fez, but I can't *believe* Demetrius slapped you," Gertie said, pulling a top hat off a rack and frisbee-ed it into the air, catching it on its way down.

"He didn't slap me, though," Bridget said.

"He did in some timelines!"

Bridget waited for her sister to calm down. "You know what he's like," Bridget said. "And it's a once in a lifetime kind of hat."

"I know."

"How are you going to feel when he sells it to someone else?"

Gertie groaned.

"So forget that he doesn't think ahead sometimes and buy it, ok?"

Gertie grumbled and nodded.

They heard barking, and Ziggy came speeding toward them. At least that's what Gertie saw. Bridget could also see the little ghost of a rat, squealing and zooming past them as it was chased, thanks to her magic eye.

"Ziggy! Heel!" Bridget called, and the dog halted in mid-air, whining as he hovered just above the ground at Bridget's side.

"Since we're here, you should get something yourself," Gertie said, holding up a flowery bonnet.

Bridget laughed. "Come on, let's go."

They returned to the check out, where Demetrius was sorting through receipts and entering information in a spreadsheet.

"I wanted to ask you something, if you're done pouting," Demetrius said, glancing up.

Gertie stuck her tongue out at the phrasing.

"Okay. Are you done *now*?" he asked.

"Yes." Gertie crossed her arms.

"My last shelf-stacker quit to go off to college." Demetrius folded a receipt and placed it in a box. "I was thinking, since you like hats almost as much as I do-"

"More than you do."

"Not a chance." Demetrius responded without looking up. "I was thinking you could start working some shifts here. I'd pay you, and maybe, once you get your apprenticeship license, I can start teaching you to enchant hats."

Gertie's mouth hung open, half forming words that she couldn't put together.

For the first time ever, Bridget saw her sister unable to think of something to say. "She'd love that," Bridget said.

Gertie nodded dumbly.

"Also, she'll take the hat."

Gertie pulled out her debit card and handed it to Demetrius.

He swiped the card and handed it back with the receipt, and pushed over the fez in its blue box. "Now get out of here before I change my mind. Text me the hours you'd be available."

"Thank you," Gertie said. She pulled the fez out and put it on her head.

✿ ✿ ✿

"I can't believe that just happened," Gertie said, nearly skipping down the sidewalk, the hatbox under her arm.

"You mean spending your life savings on a single purchase?" Bridget said with a grin. "I believe it."

"You're just jealous you can't travel through time."

"Well, when you think about it, neither can you-"

There was a now-familiar flash, and someone grabbed Bridget out of the way of a tall, gaunt woman carrying a box of glassware.

"Gertie!" the new Gertie shouted.

"Right, sorry!" Old Gertie pulled on the fez's tassel, disappearing.

The woman scowled at the girls, not knowing how her wine glasses had just been saved, and continued on her way.

"As I was saying," Gertie finished. "You're just jealous."

Bridget smiled. "Maybe a little."

Gertie and Bridget go on holiday

Bridget heaved her suitcase onto what she declared "her" bed and dropped herself down next to it. She threw her sweater (which she had been forced to remove in the airport due to the heat) onto the floor, and let out a long, contented sigh.

"Thanks for the offer, sis, but I got this." Gertie said sarcastically as she dragged her suitcase into their room and left it at the foot of her bed. In her other hand was a black and white portable hatbox, and inside sat her most prized possession - her storage hat. Using magic, it held her entire collection, stored in rows and rows of individual hat boxes.

"You're fine," Bridget responded, and unzipped her suitcase to change into shorts.

Spring in the family's home state of Tornstead was barely warmer than winter, and for this reason the family took the time to escape the chilly weather and bask in the sun of Lucembrine. The island state was famous for its beaches and sun, aquariums for the young, and wine tasting for the adults.

The cottage they had rented had a large kitchen, two bedrooms ("If you start snoring again, I won't hesitate to throw a pillow at you," Gertie had told Bridget. "Like it would reach," she'd retorted with a playful grin), two full bathrooms, and - most importantly - a beach right out the back door.

"A TV!" Gertie declared upon opening the ornate dresser that was taller than she was. She sat on her bed and clicked it on.

Theodore Mallon, their father, walked into the room to find his daughters watching an episode of a pirate cartoon.

"Did we really travel all this way just for you two to watch TV?" he asked.

"It's Lucembrine TV dad!" Gertie protested.

"It's totally different," Bridget added jokingly.

He sighed. "Isn't that what you do when you're at school?"

"At school we do homework." Bridget said, rising up on her elbows to get a better angle of the TV. "And basketball, and studying."

"And magic," Gertie added.

Their dad rubbed his forehead. "Do I have to hear about that here?"

"Well," Gertie explained. "We don't have a TV at school."

Eloise, the girls' mother, slipped into the room and put her hands on Theodore's shoulders. "Can't we just have a nice family vacation?" she asked everyone.

"That's what we're here for," the girls said in unison and laughed.

"We're going to get settled in," Eloise said, pulling her husband out the bedroom door before he could protest again.

A dog appeared in the cartoon, barking in the sunlight on the pirate's ship.

Bridget sighed. "I miss Ziggy."

"Yeah, well, he wouldn't be able to cross the ocean," Gertie said. Ghosts always had problems with salt, even when dissolved. It was why Ziggy, their ghost dog, hated popcorn and pretzels. "Besides, dad would blow a gasket."

"So would the government of Lucembrine," Bridget pointed out.

Gertie shrugged. "Dad's scarier," she joked.

The TV flickered and the lights in the room dimmed for a minute.

"Mom!" Gertie shouted. "There's something wrong with the TV!"

"And lights!" Bridget added.

Their dad appeared in the door again.

"Yes, that's why we got such a good deal," he flapped the shirt he had been in the middle of hanging, trying to get rid of the wrinkles. "Apparently there've been some intermittent electrical issues. Nothing dangerous, of course."

Gertie balked. "We're all gonna die."

❀ ❀ ❀

Later that evening, after returning to the house from a nearby aquarium, Gertie was enjoying the second to last book in the *Flowers of Dark Meadow* series, and Bridget was scrolling through the latest in sports news, when her skin itched in the way that meant something magical was nearby. She scanned the room, looking to see if there was something her spelled left eye could see that her normal right eye couldn't.

And there it was.

"Gertie..." she said, closing her laptop.

Gertie shushed her. "I'm at a good point let me just-"

"Gertie."

"I have to finish this chapter-"

"GERTIE!" Bridget shouted, pulling the book from her hands.

"Okay, okay," Gertie sat up. "What?"

"There's a ghost in here." Bridget flicked her eyes back to the corner of the room. The spirit glared back at her, his ghostly form shivering in anger. "One on the verge of becoming a poltergeist from the look of it."

Gertie sighed and grabbed her laptop from her backpack. "Ok, let's hope the Wi-Fi doesn't crap out on us."

❈ ❈ ❈

On her way to the rental car with Theodore, Eloise realized she had forgotten her purse and turned back to the cottage. She was ready to grab it from the kitchen counter and head back out. Instead, she found her daughters sitting cross legged on the floor with salt sprinkled around them in a big oval. A black top hat sat upside down in between them.

"What are you doing?" she asked.

Gertie panicked. "Nothing!"

"Weren't you going to the grocery store?" Bridget asked, trying to be more subtle.

Eloise crossed her arms. "I forgot my purse."

"Oh," Bridget glanced up. "Well, it's right there on the counter so you can just-"

"Girls."

"There's a poltergeist," Gertie said.

"An almost-poltergeist," Bridget corrected.

"The only licensed handler open during the holiday is two hours away," Gertie explained, "and his prices are way above the quality of work he provides, according to his online reviews."

Eloise couldn't believe was she was hearing. "So you decided to take care of it yourselves?"

Gertie bounced a bit in place. "I'm going to try out the ghost therapy hat that Great Grandpa Gregory gave me!"

"You *know* it's illegal to practice magic without a proper license in Lucembrine right?" Eloise asked.

Gertie and Bridget looked at each other.

"*You're* licensed," Bridget said.

Gertie nodded. "That's why I was even able to get my collection here in the first place. If you were here when we were practicing then technically..."

Eloise's cell phone rang. It was Theodore.

"Hi honey," she said after answering. "I'm actually going to spend some time with the girls. You go on ahead."

"Is there anything else we need?" Theodore asked on the other side of the call.

Eloise looked back at the salt circle her daughters were drawing for her. "Salt."

With their mother satisfactorily safe inside another salt circle, the girls sat back within theirs. Gertie checked the label on the seam of the hat again, going over the incantation one more time. She placed the hat just outside the circle of salt, so the spirit wouldn't be barred from entering it.

"Squirth oo flithum wendri'or plepp!"

The hat lit up from the inside, creating a blue spotlight on the ceiling of the cottage. There was a sucking sound, like a vacuum that had gotten stuck on a pencil. Bridget watched as the ghost, spying on them from the ceiling, got sucked down into the hat.

The blue spotlight switched off, and the hat's ribbon glowed eggshell white.

"Perfect!" Gertie said. She promptly stood and stepped out of the salt circle. Before Eloise could stop her, she scooped the hat up and placed it on her head.

Her face twisted into the expression that Bridget had seen the malevolent spirit wear.

"Oh, look what you've done now," she said with a grimace, staring down at herself. "What is this foolishness?"

"Hi," Bridget said to Gertie, trying to get the spirit that had possessed her sister to focus on her. "My name is Bridget. What's your name?"

Gertie's head snapped up to glare at Bridget. "Bartholomew Barbill. What are you doing in my house?"

Bridget swallowed nervously. "My family rented this cottage for the week."

"Well, you're not welcome here," the spirit said, making Gertie plop her fists at her waist. "No one is! This is the Barbill house. I don't know why we've had so many strangers lately-"

"The owner of this house…" Bridget looked over to her mom.

"Anthony Barbill," Eloise supplied.

"Has been renting it out-"

"Ridiculous!" the ghost said. "The Barbills have lived here for centuries! I grew up in this house! We are not leaving."

"I think you already have," Bridget said.

"No, we have not. If you will kindly pack your things, I'm sure my family will be back soon."

Eloise handed Bridget her phone. On the screen was an email from Anthony Barbill.

I'm so glad you're interested in the Barbill House, it read. *My family has been living there for centuries. It's a wonderful place, just a bit small for my three kids, my husband and I. We've since relocated. I have such wonderful memories of the house from my childhood; I'm sure you'll have a lovely time.*

The rest of the email detailed information about the beach and the steps required to rent.

Bridget handed the phone to Gertie, who read it angrily, before her expression melted into one of pain.

"Then where are they?" Bartholomew asked. "Where did they move?"

Bridget looked to her mother.

"I think their office was in Braewight, on the mainland," Eloise said, she motioned to the business cards on the countertop.

Gertie strode over and picked one up, staring at it.

The lights flickered.

"Bartholomew?" Bridget said softly.

Gertie's hand crushed the card.

"Why?" Bartholomew cried, dropping onto all fours.

Tears streamed from Gertie's eyes. Electricity started sparking around her, a sign of the ghost's pain and anger. She pounded the floor as Bartholomew screamed in anguish.

The lights flared white hot before turning off all together.

"Mom?" Bridget shouted, over the noise of the ghost's tantrum.

Eloise strode over to Gertie and pulled the hat from her head, releasing Bartholomew's spirit.

The sparking around her stopped, and Gertie looked around, bewildered. She wiped the tears from her face as the lights came back on.

"Where'd he go?" she asked.

Bridget scanned the room. Suddenly there were crashes from upstairs - he was in the attic.

Eloise and the girls pulled on a string attached to the trap door in the ceiling of the kitchen, extending a ladder for them to climb up.

Cardboard boxes were overturned, a lamp with a glass shade was shattered, and in the middle of the room a photo album lay open.

Bridget could see the ghost weeping, caressing the faces of his descendants in the pictures.

"They left me behind," he whimpered. "All I did was protect them. Help them. And they didn't even say goodbye."

"I'm so sorry," Bridget said.

"All I ever wanted was my family to be safe," Bartholomew said. "I can't move on."

"We could bring him back with us," Gertie suddenly said as the thought occurred to her, though she couldn't hear what Bartholomew was saying like Bridget could. But she had felt his pain, and knew how to help.

"What?" Bartholomew looked up with renewed hope.

"What?" Eloise snapped.

"Yeah," Gertie said, not withering a bit at her mother's glare. "Ghosts can't cross salt water, but if he's in the hat and I'm wearing the hat, then he'd probably be safe with - well - *in* me. And we're going back to the mainland. He'd have to travel a while to find his family but-" Gertie shivered, her teeth clacking together.

Bartholomew, in his joy, had embraced her.

"That's just Bartholomew, hugging you," Bridget told Gertie, explaining the sudden chill.

"Oh." Gertie awkwardly held her arms up, trying to hug him back.

Eloise sighed, knowing that once her girls came up with an idea, it was exhausting to dissuade them. Besides, on the scale of their previous exploits, this rated as "extremely safe."

Everyone froze as the locked front doorknob struggled to twist.

"Honey! Can you get the door?" Came Theodore's call from downstairs.

The three humans scrambled down the ladder.

Eloise grabbed a broom and quickly swept all the salt into a corner. Gertie shoved the ladder back up into the ceiling, coughing at the dust that fell down as a result. Bridget ran to their room and clicked on the television so it looked like they were all busy.

"What about me?" Bartholomew asked Bridget, panicked.

"He can't see you!" Bridget whispered back.

"Oh, right!"

Eloise opened the door for her husband to the sound of their daughters laughing in front of the opening credits to the movie *Melody Hill*.

"Movie's just about to start, love," Eloise said, kissing Theodore on the cheek. "Want to join us?"

Theodore sighed. "Sure, why not?"

To be continued...

Gertie and Bridget go to the beach

It was a hot day.

A sticky, sweaty, miserable day in Lucembrine where sunlight blazed and sources of shade were few and far between. An afternoon where the asphalt seemed to sizzle, concrete blinded pedestrians, and door handles fried anyone silly enough to touch them.

It was the perfect day, according to Gertie, for the beach.

Gertie and Bridget's parents were off at a wine tasting, a common tourist tradition in Lucembrine, while Bridget and Gertie had walked down the beach outside their rented cottage to a nearby boardwalk.

Gertie took to the ocean as fast as she could. She was wearing an enchanted swim cap that made her able to hold her breath longer, and she was off flaunting that ability and exploring some cave nearby.

Bridget, meanwhile, had suffered a severe sunburn the previous day of their vacation and was still feeling it on her back and shoulders. Instead of exposing herself, she sat on one of the wooden benches next to the row of shops on the boardwalk. She had a book that Gertie had lent her open on her lap, a big floppy hat that Gertie had insisted she wear ("It's enchanted to protect you from the sun!") on her head, and wore long shorts and a cardigan over a tank top to cover the burn.

She wasn't reading the book though. She was staring out at the ocean, watching it sparkle. Her ruined eye, unable to see normally since she was a child, could see many things it shouldn't. Ghosts, hidden doorways, and past the magical things people used to seem more glamorous in this setting, where they were on display. Sunscreen that gave the appearance of a perfect tan. Hair spray that formed perfect, luscious waves. Swimsuits that cast an illusion of a more fit body were the most popular.

There was also a giant sea monster in the distance, hiding under an invisibility spell among the ocean waves. Its giant eyes stared at the shore. Bridget was trying to figure out if its intentions were sinister. Most magical creatures respected living beings that weren't their natural prey. But sometimes there was a rare exception.

Something invisible appeared out of the water, and Bridget gasped. It was a little sea monster. Two tall eyestalks with tiny blinking eyes, a small squishy body and lots of tentacles. The larger monster must have been watching out for it. It scurried from the ocean and up the beach, dodging any feet that came its way.

Bridget watched with rapt attention. As it got closer, Bridget realized its destination.

An ice cream shop. It was a bar, with a green and yellow awning protecting it from the elements. The last parent and child pair in line had just been helped, and the young sea monster was heading right for it.

Discreetly, Bridget put her book in her bag and stepped up behind the monster.

The shopkeeper didn't seem to notice the little creature, for all that it was hopping up and down, waving its tentacles, trying to get her attention. Bridget hoped that the owner did know the monster, and she wasn't about to do something incredibly stupid.

Bridget knelt just behind the invisible monster.

"Excuse me," she said, after making sure no one else was around. "Would you like some assistance?"

The little thing nodded its eyestalks and held its tentacles up. Bridget picked it up and gave it her forearm for it to stand on.

"Oh!" The shopkeeper said, surprised and delighted at the little beast. "Hello there! I'm sorry I didn't see you." She pushed her sunglasses up her nose, and Bridget saw the twinkle of an enchantment on their lenses to let her see past the invisibility spell.

"What would you like?" Bridget asked, and the monster slapped a tentacle onto the glass, pointing to rocky road.

"All right," the shopkeeper said with a smile as she scooped the ice cream. "Would you like anything?" she asked Bridget.

"No, thank you," Bridget said.

The shopkeeper handed over the cone and the little monster took it in both its tentacles. Its mouth - a giant hole full of teeth - opened right under its eyestalks, and it ate the cone in one gulp.

Bridget's eyes widened and she froze at the sight of all those fangs, but the beastie didn't notice.

The monster rubbed its closed eyeball against Bridget's cheek and hopped out of her arms. She watched as it waddled down to the water and jumped into the waves.

Bridget looked to the shopkeeper, who was humming and cleaning the glass.

"Let me pay for the ice cream," she said, reaching into her bag for her wallet.

"Oh no." The woman took off her glasses, revealing two holes in her human skin suit. Eyestalks came out, and she opened her mouth to smile, and revealed the same sharp pointed teeth. "It's no charge for my nephew."

Gertie and Bridget return from holiday

"It's just an x-ray, Bartholomew, be quiet!" Bridget hissed at the ghost possessing Gertie. Her sister, or rather Bartholomew, let out a frustrated huff.

"It's so strange..." he said, staring at the screen that was revealing the contents of checked luggage. The agent weighing and taking their suitcases raised his eyebrows, but didn't say anything.

"This is a terrible idea," Eloise, Bridget and Gertie's mother, murmured. Theodore, the girls' father, was in the bathroom but could come back at any moment. He knew nothing of the sisters' plan to get Bartholomew to the mainland, and if he did there was no way he'd approve of his daughters using magic to do so.

Using a ghost therapy hat that contained his spirit and allowed for safe possession, Bartholomew was walking around using Gertie's body, gaping at cars, marveling at skyscrapers, and staring bug-eyed at airplanes as they descended into the airport.

Somehow, Theodore hadn't noticed the odd behavior yet.

"Alright, ready for security?" Theodore asked on his return, clapping his hand on Gertie's shoulder.

Bartholomew flinched, unused to how such a thing would feel in a human body.

"What?" Theodore jerked back, hurt.

"Just sunburn, dad," Bridget said.

Bartholomew nodded Gertie's head and rubbed the shoulder demonstratively.

Since they were leaving the state of Lucembrine instead of entering, they didn't need to enter a special line to declare magical items as they had on the way in. Lucembrine was very strict about magical use, much more than in the rest of the country. The family of four, plus a ghost, merely waited in line, placed their items on a conveyer belt to be x-rayed, and walked through a metal detector.

"Excuse me, miss?" A security agent held out her hand to stop Gertie.

"Uh…" Bartholomew was still getting used to the fact that he was in a female body, and would be referred to as such. "Yes, ma'am?"

"Your hat?"

"What?"

"Place your hat on the conveyor belt."

Bartholomew shot a look toward Bridget, but she nodded. It's not like they had another option. Bartholomew removed the hat.

Gertie instantly regained control over her body. It felt like she had suddenly been jolted from a dream, and she was a bit disoriented.

The security agent was getting annoyed. "Please place the hat on the conveyor belt and continue through the metal detector."

"Of course." Gertie put the hat down and watched as the ribbon turned from white to gray, signaling that Bartholomew had left the hat. "Sorry. I'm a bit sleep deprived."

She stepped through the metal detector without incident, and picked up the hat and her carry-on again.

Once they reached their gate, and their parents had settled into seats to wait, Bridget cleared her throat.

"I have to go to the bathroom," she said pointedly.

"Me too," Gertie said. "Let's go."

If Theodore thought it was strange that Gertie brought her hat with her and left her backpack, he didn't comment on it.

❉ ❉ ❉

Theodore and Eloise waited, growing anxious as announcements were made of the plane's impending departure.

"They're taking a while in there, aren't they?" Theodore asked.

Suddenly, the girls came running back, panting, Gertie with the enchanted hat back on her head.

"The bathroom was just around the corner, wasn't it?" Theodore asked suspiciously.

Gertie and Bridge glanced at each other, having just had to search the entire area near security and the surrounding gates before finding Bartholomew invisibly staring at a vending machine in wonder.

"I had too much coffee," Bridget finally mumbled, staring at the ground.

Theodore threw up his hands. "I don't need to know any more."At the same time, Gertie and Bridget's phones started buzzing.

"Oh, Ernest posted a new song," Bridget said, clicking on the notification. A video of Ernest performing with his guitar popped up, and Gertie's eyes nearly bugged out of her head.

"How is that...?" Bartholomew stumbled over his words, remembering that Gertie's parents were still present.

Bartholomew-in-Gertie pulled her phone from her pocket, staring at it. He clicked on the notification to reveal the video, like Bridget had. He touched the phone and the page took that to mean he wanted to scroll, and Bartholomew found himself looking at the handful of responses to the video. Most of them were negative.

Gertie sucked in a breath.

"Such language!" Bartholomew said.

Bridget laughed nervously. "Nothing we haven't seen before, though," she added awkwardly.

Theodore narrowed his eyes at his daughters, but the boarding process began, and he and Eloise started paying attention to that instead.

"What else can this magic thing do?" Bartholomew asked, holding the phone up in front of Bridget.

"It's actually mostly not magic," she said. "Science has come a long way."

Bartholomew's eyes widened, and the Mallon family's section number was called.

"Let's go!" Eloise said, grabbing Theodore's hand to lead the family, shoving past other passengers on their way to the line.

Gertie looked queasy as the family got closer to the door to the ramp, and by the time she reached the front of the line and handed over her ticket, her forehead was visibly glistening with sweat.

"Are you alright, miss?" The flight attendant asked.

"Yes!" Bartholomew blurted. "I am fine. There's nothing wrong."

"Are you sure?" The flight attendant paused in handing back the ticket.

Bridget put a calming hand on Gertie's shoulder.

"She's just a little nervous about flying," Bridget said. "Once we get on the plane, she'll be fine. She falls right to sleep."

The flight attendant seemed to think that was good enough, and let the family board.

Gertie sat in the window seat, hugged her knees to her chest, and started a low whine.

"Gertie!" Bridget hissed. When Bartholomew didn't answer, she elbowed her. "Bart!"

"Why am I doing this?" Bartholomew moaned. "What if it doesn't work? I've never, ever left Lucembrine, not even when I was alive!"

Theodore settled in next to the girls before Eloise could stop him, and noticed Gertie's vulnerable state.

"What's the matter?" he asked. "Are you feeling okay?"

Gertie nodded, but she wasn't fooling anyone.

"You haven't had problems flying in years," Theodore said, reaching over Bridget to put a hand on Gertie's arm. "It's going to be okay. It will be over before you know it."

"Thanks...Dad," Gertie said.

"If you'll all put your seat backs and trays in their upright and locked position, and turn off any electrical or magical devices, we'll be taking off shortly," came a voice over the PA system.

"Where did that come from?" Bartholomew mused, staring at the ceiling of the plane in confusion.

Theodore opened his mouth to ask about the strange question from his daughter, when Eloise animatedly gestured to the screens they had on the back of the chairs in front of them from across the aisle. "Look Teddy! They have free poker! Let's play!"

Gertie was all but hyperventilating as the plane began rolling away from the gate. "What if I get left behind?" he whispered to Bridget.

She didn't have an answer for him.

The engines began to growl, and Bartholomew held his breath.

The plane started racing down the runway, and Bridget gripped Gertie's hand.

The aircraft lifted, and they were flying over the land. When they crossed the ocean, they would have their answer. Gertie and Bridget anxiously looked out the window, watching as the plane left the airport and was over the ocean.

As soon as the glimmering blue shone up at her, Bridget turned to stare at Gertie, waiting for something to happen.

Gertie looked down at the ocean, and up at her sister.

"It's working!" Bartholomew whispered. "I'm still here!"

The girls hugged in triumph.

Theodore smiled over at them.

"It really is nice that they're so close," he mused to Eloise.

She just nodded. "Full house," she said, pointing at the screen again.

❁ ❁ ❁

It was a six hour flight, and before long the Mallons had all fallen asleep. All except Bartholomew. There was no way he was missing a second of it.

Bartholomew nudged Bridget awake as the plane started to descend. "Something's wrong with her ears!" he whispered.

Bridget yawned. "It's just the change in altitude. You're fine."

"So your sister's not dying?"

Bridget shook her head.

"Oh. Alright then."

The plane touched down with a rumble. They taxied into the gate, and Bartholomew was almost jumping up and down in the chair. He was going to see his family again! He fixed the image of the map that Bridget had shown him in his mind. He would find them.

The family shuffled off the plane, all sore and tired.

"Can I go to the bathroom?" Bridget asked.

"Can't you wait until we get home?" Theodore countered.

Eloise nudged him. "It'll only take them a few minutes."

"Them?"

"I have to go too," Bartholomew-in-Gertie hurriedly said. They headed toward the nearest bathroom.

After making sure it was empty, Bridget stood against the door to allow for privacy.

Bartholomew turned to face her.

"I will never be able to thank you and your sister enough," he said. "Can you please pass on my sincerest thanks to her?"

"Of course."

Bartholomew nodded.

"Goodbye." He put both of Gertie's hands on the brim of the hat and pulled up.

Gertie blinked. The last thing she had known, she was back in the airport using the incantation to get Bartholomew back into the hat.

"*That's* the way to travel," she murmured to herself.

Bridget watched Bartholomew wave, smiling. He walked through the wall of the bathroom, heading west toward where his family was.

"Uh, Bridget?"

"Yeah?" Bridget turned toward her sister, glad to have her back.

"Is it okay if I actually go to the bathroom?" Gertie asked. "It was a really long flight, and I don't think Bartholomew remembered how."

Gertie and Bridget go on a tour

As Gertie and Bridget were walking from breakfast to their first classes, they were greeted by a group of teens and adults blocking the path between buildings.

"Oh great," Bridget said. "A tour."

Most prospective students to Flories Boarding School would fly out for a day of pre-scheduled activities designed to make the campus an attractive alternative to normal day schools. For the teens, the freedom angle of the dorms was played up, while reiterating curfew and the presence of residential advisors so the parents would approve.

Bridget and Gertie groaned, trying to get around the group and being blocked at every turn by a parent taking pictures or a younger sibling getting distracted by a row of flowers, a statue, or an ivy covered building.

"Are there any magical clubs here?" a boy with a curly mess of hair and thick rimmed glasses asked the tour guide.

Gertie almost stopped, but Bridget found an opening between a set of families and pulled her through.

"No," the tour guide said. At the boy's obvious disappointment, she recovered quickly. "But there's nothing stopping you from starting one!"

"That won't be necessary," the boy's father said, and his mother nodded grimly.

Gertie frowned as they left. Another magic aficionado whose dreams were crushed by their parents.

In the middle of Bridget's advanced calculus class, the tour group squeezed in, filling the entire front corner of the class by the door and spilling back into the hall.

"Hi Mr. Terkin," the tour guide said. "Sorry to interrupt."

"No problem, Lauren," Mr. Terkin said.

Bridget took a deep breath to hold in a sigh. She put her pen down and prepared herself to have to study this weekend for the midterm, since the teacher was obliged to turn his attention to the visitors.

Tour group season was the worst.

"Did any students have questions about mathematics, or any classes here?" Lauren asked the group.

"Or the swim team. I'm the coach," Mr. Terkin added.

One of the tour group members perked up. "When are tryouts?" he asked. He was tall and lean, with tan lines around his eyes that Bridget had assumed were from sunglasses. Swim goggles would also make sense, though.

"Two weeks, just after the new quarter."

The rest of the prospective students asked about things like class sizes and available electives.

"Next period there's an acting class," Lauren said, gathering her flock to leave the classroom as the bell rang. "I can take you to look in."

I'm sure they won't mind, Bridget thought, packing up her bag.

During their weekly afternoon assembly, Headmistress Clearwater was talking about voting for the school dance in the middle of the next quarter and Bridget noticed the tour group slipping into the back rows. Of course they'd want to see the headmistress in action.

As Gertie, Bridget, and their friend Vivien left the assembly, they passed one family in particular talking to the tour guide and Headmistress Clearwater. In it was the boy with glasses who had asked the question about clubs, the swimmer from Bridget's class, and a girl who was apparently their sister, based on the family's curly brown hair and large ears. Bridget immediately noticed, with her magic eye, that every bit of the girl's jewelry - from her multiple pairs of earrings to her three necklaces and multiple thin bracelets - was enchanted with spells. The only one she recognized was the charm on her necklace that enabled her to communicate with dogs.

"All of our teachers stress responsibility when it comes to magic," the headmistress was saying. Catching Vivien's eye, she smiled. "Maybe these students could talk to you about it?"

The three siblings and their parents looked over. Vivien flushed in embarrassment at the reference to her past mistakes.

"Sorry, we're late for study group," Gertie lied, glaring at the headmistress. The three girls hurried away, not looking back.

After dinner, the sisters were on their way to the lit, outdoor basketball courts for Bridget to get some reverse layup practice outside of her normal team practice. They passed the student center on their way; the tour was letting out after the special dinner for prospective students, where teachers were in attendance to answer any questions, have one-on-one conversations with the parents, and eat a free steak dinner. Gertie and Bridget stopped to watch the group split into individual families who headed toward the parking lot by the woods.

"Finally," Gertie said, still annoyed at the tour's presence during her lunch period.

"Maybe those practitioner ones will come back," Bridget said, dribbling the ball in place as they watched. "It'd be nice to have more people with magic here."

Gertie just shrugged, stole the ball out from under Bridget's hand and ran for the court without dribbling.

"That's traveling!" Bridget shouted, jogging to catch up.

A week later, Gertie, Bridget, Vivien and Ernest were heading to movie night when they noticed a disturbance in the alley between Gertie's dorm and the building next door. It was a favorite spot for bullies, as Gertie, Bridget and Ernest knew all too well, due to the close quarters and the lack of light.

"We should go help whoever it is," Bridget said, stretching out her shoulders in preparation for a fight.

"All right," Gertie grumbled, not having a hat with a useful enchantment for this situation on her.

Ernest pulled his piccolo pieces out from his backpack and started putting them together. His music-based magic came in handy during fights; sometimes he was even able to freeze the fighters in place. Vivien took a deep breath, trying to call up the self defense moves her gym class had instilled in her.

As they rounded the corner into the alley and their eyes adjusted, they were met with a surprising sight.

The bullies had surely been the ones to jump the new students, but they were the ones getting pummeled. Bridget and Gertie immediately recognized the new students as two of the siblings from the tour group.

The tall swimmer dodged a punch from one of the bullies - Jodie Migaran, one of Bridget's least favorite teammates - but still caught her knee in his side. He recovered from the impact, reached up, grabbed Jodie, and shoved her against the wall with lightning fast speed that could only come from a spell. Jodie ducked as he curled his fist for a blow and he ended up punching the wall.

He groaned in pain, holding his hand up to reveal broken fingers. But as Gertie and Bridget watched, the bones righted themselves, healing in a matter of seconds.

Jodie jumped and kicked at his ribs, sending him into the opposite wall. She stood panting for a moment, while Nick Coffer - another bully well known to Bridget, Gertie and Vivien - started punching his face. The swimmer jabbed Nick in the gut, sending him gasping for air, and ran to tackle Jodie. He slammed her into the opposite alley wall.

When she landed, the bricks of the alley shifted and twisted into branches that reached out to curl around her.

"Hey!" she shouted, being pulled against the wall.

Gertie looked for the source of the magic, and caught the boy with the glasses waving his hands and casting spells in a magical language unfamiliar to her.

Nick ran toward the caster, trying to break his focus on his magic. Instead, he fell foot first into a deep shaft of water, courtesy of the brother's magic changing the ground into liquid.

Two of the bullies' friends ran away after that, one nursing a bleeding nose and the other having had his baseball bat turned into a long loaf of bread.

Satisfied that he wouldn't be attacked again, the caster reached into the water, pulled Nick halfway out, and yanked a hair from the bully's head. He unceremoniously dropped Nick back in after he managed to get a few gasping breaths.

The boy with the glasses then moved on to Jodie. After making sure her hands were secured by the branches, he plucked one of her long blond hairs and took a step back.

"Listen to me carefully, so you can tell your friends," he said, speaking calmly, like this happened all the time. "I'm going to use these to cast a spell on my brother and me. If you try to hurt either of us again, anything you do to us will happen to you too."

Jodie struggled against the branches.

The caster pocketed the hairs and backed away. "You can try to convince some other friends to try, but..." He stepped aside to reveal Nick thrashing to the surface of the shaft.

Jodie broke free of the branches and reached into the water.

She pulled a gasping Nick up, soaking herself in the process.

"I'm alright," Nick said through chattering teeth.

Jodie helped Nick stand, and together they limped past Gertie, Bridget, Vivien and Ernest, not even sparing a glance in their direction.

The brothers looked at each other for a breath and then at Gertie and Bridget's group.

"Hi," the boy with the glasses said. "We seem to have gotten lost." He smiled, which somehow made Bridget feel all the more uneasy. "Any chance you can point us to the Meirgorge dorms?"

Gertie's mouth opened and closed, still surprised by what she had seen.

"Sorry," he said, running a hand through his curly hair. "We should introduce ourselves. I'm Charlie Nessing, and this is my older brother Peter. We're just moving in."

The swimmer nodded and held up his hand in a wave. It moved like it had never been broken.

Gertie and Bridget join a club

"COME JOIN THE MAGIC CLUB," read big, bold letters on a flyer pinned to the dorm bulletin board, impossible for Gertie to miss even before her morning tea.

Meeting in faculty sponsor Mr. Jerson's room, Haste 209, Fridays from 4-5. Don't have to bring anything but yourselves! Sincerely, Club President Charlie Nessing.

❊ ❊ ❊

Gertie managed to drag Bridget and Ernest along with her to the meeting, while Vivien came willingly.

"It's those guys who beat up Jodie and Nick and their group," Ernest said. "Do we really need more bullies in our lives?"

"Maybe there will be others who are interested in magic," Gertie argued. "Wouldn't it be nice to have more friends?"

Gertie wore a black, wide-brimmed hat that she wore to functions where entertainment was key. The flyer didn't state to bring any magical demonstrations, but she figured it wouldn't hurt.

As they walked, she practiced releasing colorful sparks from her hands, using the powers granted to her by the hat. She even managed to shape them into a heart before they fizzled away.

Some other students were in Mr. Jerson's room already - a few that Gertie recognized, but most she had never seen. Gertie ignored the urge to sit in her assigned seat, and sat in the front row with her friends.

"Nice to see you here," Mr. Jerson, her Potions teacher, said to her, his smile wrinkling the corners of his eyes.

Gertie nodded, nervous energy coming out in drumbeats from her fingertips.

More students filtered in as the clock ticked on. Marissa Hanler, a straight A student, came and sat in front, begging to be noticed by Mr. Jerson. Darryl Fudin, another classmate, came in and sat behind Gertie.

"I thought you'd be here too," he said with a grin.

"I didn't know you would!" she said, pleased that her potions tutoring had seemed to actually plant a seed of interest in magic.

"I mean, I have *plenty* of time in my schedule," he said sarcastically. "What's one more after-school activity? I can sneak pizza into the computer lab so I don't have to eat while running to football practice."

All together, the club consisted of about twenty-five members. Gertie beamed. There were so many people interested in magic! Who knew?

Then came two of the new students Ernest had worried about: Peter and Faye Nessing. Faye quickly chose a desk off to the side. She placed her backpack underneath, pulled out a book, opened to a bookmark and started reading. Bridget frowned. An animal anatomy textbook? What high school freshman needed to know that?

"Peter, good to see you," Mr. Jerson said. "Where's your brother?"

The tall senior slicked back his hair - still wet from swim practice - and shrugged. "I'm sure he's coming, sir. We can probably start introductions without him?"

Mr. Jerson nodded his approval.

Peter stood at the front of the class.

"Hi, everyone. Thank you for coming. My name is Peter Nessing, and I'm the Vice President of the Magic Club." He fidgeted with a charm on a leather necklace. "Let's see. I'm a senior. My siblings and I just started school here last week. Fun fact about me is that I've been accepted to Wespire University on a swimming scholarship - I'm on the swim team here too - and I'm going to study Business. How about we-"

The classroom's phone pealed, loud and irritating, until Mr. Jerson answered it.

"Yes?"

He listened for a moment, his hand gripping the receiver harder and harder as the person on the other side spoke to him.

"I'll be right there," he said. He stood and addressed the club. "There's a little...problem in the healer's office. They need some help brewing a proper potion."

Mr. Jerson hesitated, trying to decide if he should tell the students to leave.

"I can handle it, sir," Peter said. "We'll just do introductions and take down some suggestions for club activities."

Mr. Jerson nodded. "I'll be back as soon as I can."

As soon as he left, there was murmuring about what could be going wrong in the healer's office.

"Jodie Migaran threw up in fifth period," someone whispered. "I wonder if it could have anything to do with that?"

"What? Nick did too. He seriously looked green!"

"Okay, everyone." Peter held up his hands. "There's no reason to speculate. As I was saying-"

Suddenly Charlie, the middle Nessing sibling, burst into the room.

"I need help!" he shouted.

"What?" Peter frowned. He looked over his brother as he came to the front of the class, searching for injury. "What's wrong?"

Charlie pulled his backpack off his shoulder. He unzipped it and turned it over, dumping notebooks, pencils, and a strange golden box onto the demonstration table in the front of the classroom.

The box was tied with twine that glimmered with an enchantment. It was clearly the only thing keeping the box closed, as the flip lid struggled to open, rattling ominously.

"What is it?" someone asked.

"I don't know!" Charlie's eyes were wide and panicked. He gestured to the box wildly. "It was just...in my suitcase! I was unpacking and it just started shaking!"

"What's the string?" Darryl asked.

"Just some store-bought trap twine." Charlie pushed his thick rimmed glasses up his nose. "It's all I had. The enchantment's not going to hold very long."

The box jumped into the air, the lid struggling against the twine.

"What's in there?" Peter got closer to the box, staring at it.

"I have no idea!"

"Have you tried a Sparkness circle?" Vivien asked. "It's a good generic containment spell."

"Of course I tried that already." Charlie rolled his eyes. "My parents invented it."

"Your parents what?" Gertie repeated.

"They work at Sparkslab," Peter supplied. "Well, they did until recently. Our dad quit to run for Mayor. They've invented tons of stuff."

A student reached to peek into the box, curious about what was inside. The box opened as far as it could given the twine, and orange goop sprayed all over the place, covering the student and those behind him.

"Uck! What is this?" the student sniffed at his shirt and made a face.

"I know, it's gross!" Charlie wrinkled his nose. "I was able to get it off with some nail polish remover I borrowed from one of my floor-mates."

Those hit with the sludge left, struggling to wipe off the stickiness with towels from the potions lab, smelling like overripe fruit.

"You know..." Marissa stood, grabbing her backpack. "This isn't what I signed up for. Not when Mr. Jerson didn't even mention anything about extra credit. I have homework to do.

Good luck with the box."

She hurried out of the classroom, following the other students.

Vivien traced over one of the symbols etched into the gold side of the box. "Wait, I know this!" she said. She pulled her laptop from her bag and started searching. "It's a newer magical dialect. I researched it when looking into homunculi."

"Homunculi?" Charlie repeated.

Vivien nodded, oblivious to his approval.

Gertie looked over her shoulder, kneeling next to her desk. "We can translate it. Maybe it's a spell that will help?"

Charlie nodded. "Please, anything."

The box rattled in place, as if it was worried it was being forgotten.

"I wonder what's even in there," Bridget mused. "If it could cause us danger, I would think I'd see a vision of it."

"Did you say 'vision'?" Peter asked.

Bridget flushed, annoyed she had let it slip. The other students, debating what to do with the box, didn't seem to notice. "Yeah. I sometimes get visions," she said.

"That's amazing!" Peter said.

To his surprise, Bridget shrugged and pulled out her phone, seemingly disinterested in coming up with a way to make the box safe.

"If there's something alive in there, maybe I can calm it down," Ernest said. He started to whistle a tune, and the box started rattling harder.

It wasn't the only thing. Faye's backpack starting jumping into the air.

"What's that?" Darryl asked. "A magic backpack?"

The flap fell open revealing a rabbit with his ears pointed toward Ernest. It stumbled forward, its back leg in a cast.

"No!" Faye said. Her voice sounded odd, like it was laced with magic. Bridget watched with her enchanted eye as one of her bracelets sparked. She had recognized one of the girl's necklaces as having a charm to talk to dogs. Could she also talk to bunnies?

"You get back here!" Faye ordered the rabbit, as it hopped to Ernest. It stopped and turned back toward her ruefully, but it didn't budge.

"Faye," Peter said, a warning in his voice. "I thought you weren't supposed to bring him to class anymore."

"I'm almost finished healing him," Faye grumbled.

Ernest stopped his whistling, and the rabbit turned back to glare up at him, wanting him to finish.

"Then I'll put him back in the forest." She picked up the rabbit and put him on her desk. "Stay here."

It pouted, but laid down on its front paws, its ears and nose twitching in annoyance.

The box continued to clatter ominously.

Ernest frowned, and started whistling a different tune. There was a click as the box's two clips flipped down. The box shook, but the lid wasn't cracking open anymore.

"Nice job!" Charlie said. "You're the Yilnog right? I saw you in the yearbook."

"Yeah." Ernest shrugged. He didn't get along with the rest of his family, despite its fame as one of the oldest magical clans. It rivaled even Gertie and Bridget's, the Mallons.

"It's good to meet you!" Charlie smiled. "Music magic is a wonderful specialty. Good choice! You know your stuff."

Ernest didn't know if he'd ever heard someone compliment his skills like that before. He smiled hesitantly and nodded at Charlie.

At the first success with the box, the other students seemed to relax. They started chatting amongst each other, trading their histories with magic and their skills.

"Done!" Gertie announced, holding up the notebook that she and Vivien had been translating the box spells into. A couple club members glanced over it, admiring their work.

"Should we try it?" Vivien asked.

The box shook, daring her to.

Charlie nodded. "Maybe it'll shut it up."

Vivien gestured that Gertie should cast the spell.

Gertie waved her hands over the box, reading from the notebook, summoning the magical energy she had stored in her various keychain accessories.

At the last word, the clips flipped back up and the box lid opened, breaking the twine that had somewhat contained it.

"Uh oh," Gertie said.

It released a puff of smoke, filling the room with the noxious smell of burnt sugar. Peter tackled the box, slamming the lid shut, but the damage was done.

The other students started coughing, all clamoring to escape the room.

Including Darryl. "Sorry guys," he coughed, fleeing.

"I can fix this!" Gertie shouted, pulling her t-shirt over her nose and mouth to filter out the smoke.

She searched through the cabinets over Mr. Jerson's desk until she found a glass cup. It had a symbol etched into the side for "clean," in a magical language. It was used to clear a room of any airborne potions - and this was close enough.

She held her hand in front of the symbol and said, "Begin" in its magical language.

The smoke cleared from the room, swirling away and disappearing into the cup.

"I really should get myself one of these," Gertie said, coughing up the last of the smoke.

"Where did you *get* this box?" Vivien asked, wiping away tears from the smell.

Charlie just shrugged, looking mystified. "It was just...there. In my luggage."

"It's a joke," Bridget suddenly said, standing up. She held out her phone.

Magical A-Musings presents the Caper Carton! Confound your friends! Trick your enemies! It rattles, it shakes, it slimes and it smokes! While perfectly harmless, it is the most irritating riddle your victims will come across. Want to end the madness for them? Just press the hidden button in the back to reveal it was empty the whole time!

Bridget walked up to the box and scratched her nails against its back until she found the hidden compartment diagramed on the website. She flipped it open and pressed the bright red button.

The rattling stopped. Bridget opened the lid of the box, and nothing happened. Just as the advertisement said, it was empty.

"So who tricked you?" Bridget asked, looking up at Charlie.

"No one," Charlie mumbled. "I just...I found it. But thanks." He nodded. "Really, thank you. I wouldn't have thought to look it up. It seemed like an artifact."

The silence stretched on until Peter clapped his hands together. "Well, I think that wraps up our first club meeting," he said. "I'll send out an email and hope that *anybody* comes back."

"Will you?" Charlie asked Bridget, Gertie, Vivien and Ernest.

Bridget was hesitant, but Ernest broke into a wide grin. "Yeah! This was fun!"

Gertie nodded along. "We'll definitely be back."

❀ ❀ ❀

After everyone left, Charlie gathered up the box and the discarded twine.

"That's the first time anyone's figured out it was a cheap gag," Charlie mumbled.

Peter nodded. "But, come on, it wasn't that bad," he said. "We found some talented classmates. I think we could have a lot of fun while we're here. And two Mallons and a Yilnog? We hit the jackpot."

"There's something great about this pit of a school after all," Charlie agreed. "If they can be persuaded to bend the rules."

Faye picked up the rabbit, holding him in one hand and her textbook in the other. "You guys need to be more careful. The Potions teacher probably knows that someone magicked those bullies to be sick. He'll be on the lookout for who."

"They deserved it," Charlie muttered. "Magicless oafs."

"If you get in trouble again and it gets back to dad, we'll never hear the end of it," Faye warned.

Peter scoffed. "We don't make trouble, it finds us."

Charlie smirked. "For now."

Gertie and Bridget watch fireworks

"Hey, boy, it's okay."

The fireworks continued to thump and fizz in the background and Ziggy the ghost dog continued to whine, hiding under Gertie's bed.

"We can't even put a thunder jacket on him," Bridget said, running her hand through her long hair. "It was never this bad when he was alive."

"They were never this close when he was alive," Gertie grumbled. The fireworks were being set off in the field on campus in honor of the Flories Falcons football team, which had made it to the playoffs. Even Gertie could feel the vibration of the fireworks like a bass track cranked to its max volume.

Ziggy shivered, his whole body tense from the stress.

A spectacularly loud firework went off, echoing off the building next door and sounding like it was in the room with them.

Ziggy yelped and ran. Right through the wall and into the

hallway.

"Ziggy!" Bridget cried, yanking the door open to follow him.

Gertie ran after her, holding her baseball cap (the only thing that allowed her to see and hear their ghost dog) on her head as it threatened to bounce off.

The dog ran down the stairs, leaving the sisters even more in his dust as they were forced to pause at the doors and run slowly to keep themselves from falling down the steps.

By the time they made it out of the building, Ziggy was nowhere in sight.

"Shit!" Gertie shouted, panting from the run.

Bridget took a deep breath to calm herself, turning to look at the fireworks at her back. They were glorious, even with the trouble they had caused.

"He would've gone that way." Bridget pointed opposite of the fireworks, towards the school gate.

"What are we going to do?" Gertie asked. "Stumble around in the dark until we find him?"

"Yeah," Bridget said.

Gertie paused, gathering her resolve. "Okay. We're going to miss curfew."

"Then we miss curfew."

The sisters set off, listening for barking.

They turned toward the residential district, figuring that Ziggy would know that area better since that's where the three of them went on their walks. Stretching apartment buildings became thin three story houses, all crammed together like books on an overstuffed shelf.

Bridget nearly tripped over a cat that was on her left, the side that she was blind on because of her enchanted eye. The feline was hiding under an overturned box, and it hissed and struck out with its claws at Bridget's ankle.

"Think Ziggy scared her?" Gertie asked. Cats were often able to see the mystical, and ghosts were no exception, especially ghost dogs.

Bridget shrugged. "Let's hope so."

They moved farther away from school than they normally did. The houses they walked by became shabbier, with peeling paint and unkept lawns. Fewer cars drove by and the streetlights were frequently burned out.

"Do you feel that?" Bridget asked, a tinge of hope in her voice. A chill had come over her, like ghostly energy was near.

They rounded the corner, and sure enough, a ghost hovered over the lawn of a house in front of them. The bad news was it wasn't Ziggy.

While Gertie couldn't see anything but the yard, because her hat was spelled specifically to let her see Ziggy, Bridget's enchanted eye let her see the mystical better than a cat could. She could see the ghost of a squirrel rolling around in a bed of weeds, seemingly taken with them. Soon, another ghost - this one of a racoon - joined it, collapsing on the ground and inhaling deeply.

"The ghosts love this stuff," Bridget said, pointing to the plant. "What is it?"

Gertie pulled out her phone, leaning closer to the plant to determine its characteristics.

Suddenly a spotlight flashed on the yard. The ghost animals

bolted away as a man came running out of his house, a bat in his hands.

"Leave my house alone, you hooligans!" he shouted, and Gertie and Bridget jumped. "I'm calling the police!"

"We're not here to mess with your house," Bridget explained, her heart racing. "Our dog ran away from fireworks at the school and we're just looking for him."

The man glared. "You're telling me you're not the ones that broke in and ransacked the place?"

"No!" Bridget shook her head emphatically. "No way! We wouldn't do that! We've never been here before!"

"Someone moved things around in your house?" Gertie clarified, her eyes still locked on her phone. "Was anything stolen?"

"No," the man said. "Thankfully."

"Could the police find evidence of a break-in? Was the door kicked in? Were there pick scratches on your locks?"

"No, but-"

"Have you been experiencing electrical problems?"

The man's eyes narrowed. "How did you know that?"

"I don't think anyone broke in," Gertie said, finally looking up. She pointed to the weed. "That's a plant commonly known as ghostclover. It attracts ghosts, like flies to honey. You get someone to remove it for you, the ghosts will leave you alone."

The man gaped at her, and then at the plant.

Gertie shrugged. "You don't have to believe me. But..." Gertie hesitated, trying to decide if the man would be open to her request. "Would you mind if I took some of it with me? It'd probably make my potions teacher happy and get me some extra credit."

The man waved his hand dismissively. "Take whatever you want. I'm going back to bed."

Gertie kneeled by the weed and looked up at Bridget. "Please tell me you've got some sort of container in your bag?"

Bridget started rummaging through the messenger bag that she almost always had with her. "Are you really giving it to Mr. Jerson?" she asked, holding out a plastic zip-top bag.

Gertie took the bag and used it to pick what looked like a flower off the weed. The silver petals were actually seeds with casings like little wings to give it the ability to drift on the wind.

"No, but it sounded more legitimate than 'I want to experiment with it'." Gertie zipped up the top of the bag and stuffed it with the flower and seeds in her pocket. "Can I have another bag?" she asked Bridget, who obliged. Gertie used the new bag to grab a handful of the weeds - leaves, vines, and a few flowers.

"This should help us get Ziggy to come back with us," she said.

Bridget sighed. "Not if we don't know where he is. Let's face it, he'd never come this far."

Gertie frowned. "Where would he even run to? Where is he most comfortable?"

Bridget bit her bottom lip. When Ziggy didn't want to just sleep in one of their rooms, he would follow them to classes and through the city. If he was scared, like he was now, he'd want somewhere quiet and covered, that he knew and felt safe in.

"I know where he is!" the sisters exclaimed at the same time.

✿ ✿ ✿

"Hey boy, I brought you something," Gertie said, holding the ghostclover out. From under the statue of a scientist on a bench in the middle of Spacer Park, they could hear a sniffing noise. Ziggy's nose appeared, and then the rest of him, as he rubbed his head against the weed.

He loved this statue. When the girls came to watch street performers, he'd spend all his time hanging in the shade underneath the bronze bench.

"Ziggy!" Bridget reached down to pet him. Her hand phased into his fur instead of brushing through it, but his eyes closed in joy the same way they had when he had been alive.

Are the fireworks over? Gertie texted their friend Vivien.

Just had the grand finale. You might even make it back by curfew if you hurry.

"Let's go home," Gertie said.

Ziggy yipped in agreement.

❖ ❖ ❖

"Okay, let's try this out." Gertie held up the thunder jacket she'd enchanted using the ghostclover she had been growing in a terracotta pot on her windowsill. She wrapped it around Ziggy, buckling it under his belly. It stayed in place instead of falling through his ghostly body, and his front legs shifted to fit in the armholes.

Ziggy ran around in a circle, and the jacket stayed with him.

"Yes!" Gertie spun around in her computer chair in triumph.

"Nice work," Bridget said from Gertie's bed.

Ziggy ran up to her, showing off his new jacket and barking excitedly.

"I can make him toys now!" Gertie said excitedly, her mind whirling over the possibilities. "And gloves to really pet him with! And a leash! We could actually walk him, and play fetch, and-!"

There was a boom and blue and green lights flashed through the window. The Falcons had managed to get to the finals.

Ziggy whimpered and headed to the door. But instead of flying through it, his jacket, corporeal as it was, held him back. His legs scurried, trying to run, but he was stuck in place, looking headless to the girls.

"It's okay, Ziggy." Bridget stood and picked him up by the jacket to carry him back to the bed. "We've got you."

Bridget takes the wheel

"What's the first thing you do?" Gertie asked, sitting in the passenger seat of Vivien's minivan in the student parking lot of Flories Boarding School.

Bridget reached to push the ignition button.

Gertie caught her wrist. "No. Now you fail."

"For trying to start the car?" Bridget said.

"Yep. Try again."

Bridget looked around the car for a sign of what to do. She noticed Gertie not wearing her seatbelt.

"Let me guess. Buckle up for safety?" she asked.

Gertie smiled and nodded and clicked her seatbelt in place.

"People actually fail for that?" Bridget asked.

"Yep." Vivien leaned forward, against the back of Gertie's seat. "One of my best friends back home ranted about it for ages."

"That just seems like a trick," Bridget said.

"You are responsible for the safety of your passengers," Gertie said, in full teacher mode. "Now, pull out of the parking lot before

Vivien changes her mind."

Bridget pushed the green "start" button and the car rumbled to life. She took a deep breath to calm herself, clicked her blinker on, and pulled out of the parking spot while looking behind the car the whole time.

Vivien's minivan was purple, which made it painfully conspicuous as they drove past the school. One of the doors and the back had been painted so it acted like a chalkboard. As if the color wasn't attention-grabbing enough, Vivien had written STUDENT DRIVER in big, block letters across the side and back.

Bridget tried to ignore the unfounded nerves that people were laughing and pointing. It was much too early for anyone to be out and about.

They pulled out of the student lot, made their way along the seldom used school roads and headed out into the city. The car drove past the subway station they normally took, Mentos, the coffee shop they would hang out at, and their favorite nearby restaurants. The road was eerily devoid of company, with the exception of a bus or the occasional jogger.

"Turn left," Gertie said, and at the next light Bridget complied.

Bridget had had some lessons already, both with a professional driving instructor and with her and Gertie's dad. But she needed to get experience driving the roads she would be taking the test on, and the city of Wespire was notorious for crabby drivers and extreme traffic. The only reasonable way to have driving lessons was in the wee hours of the morning, when the roads were all but abandoned.

Bridget's eye glanced down to the speedometer and back to the road as she drove. Gertie checked, and wasn't surprised to see her sister was keeping the car exactly at the speed limit. Bridget constantly flicked her eye to her left mirror, having to turn her head a bit, to compensate for the lack of peripheral vision on that side, thanks to her ruined eye.

"Try to relax your shoulders," Vivien said, noticing Bridget's back was stiff and her knuckles white.

"I will never relax anything while driving," Bridget retorted.

"Then how are you going to get anywhere?" Gertie asked teasingly.

"Please." Bridget wrinkled her nose in disgust. "Like licenses are necessary in this day and age. How much am I *actually* going to have to drive, once I get my license? Even if we ignore buses and bikes and-"

"Change into the left lane," Gertie said.

Bridget sighed, clicked the turn signal up with her ring finger and craned her neck to get a good view.

Out of nowhere, one of the tires rumbled. Bridget gasped, unsure what to do.

Gertie's hand reached out and pressed the "self-driving" button on the dashboard. It lit up green and the car began to control itself. It put on its hazards and started pulling into the bike lane. Bridget let go of the wheel, glaring as she saw it light up with magic. She crossed her arms in defeat, and the car slowed to a stop next to the sidewalk.

"This is exactly what I'm talking about," Bridget said as Gertie opened her door.

"What do you mean?" Gertie asked, looking back to try to figure out what had happened.

"Why does the law require a licensed driver in the car!" Bridget exclaimed. "The magic driver handles emergencies much better than I ever could!"

"A car can't change it's own tire," Vivien said, her voice sounding a bit lost. She pulled the minivan's handle and her door slid open.

"Well maybe it *should*," Bridget grumbled, turning off the car and getting out.

"Oh no," Gertie whispered, just out enough into the road to see what had happened.

Bridget had hit a cat.

"No!" Bridget ran and kneeled next to the poor thing. Its eyes were closed and it wasn't moving. "No! No no no."

"It's not your fault," Gertie said, putting a comforting hand on her shoulder.

"Of course it is!" Bridget started crying, her tears falling next to the black and orange cat.

"Bridget, there was nothing you could do," Gertie said, crouching to try to meet her gaze. "None of us saw it. The same thing would have happened if either of us had been driving-"

"But you weren't!" Bridget shouted and hiccupped a sob. "I...I killed it!"

"No, you didn't," Vivien murmured, as if she was listening very intently for something no one else could hear. She kneeled next to Bridget. "It's not dead. It's dying."

"Is that any better?" Bridget asked.

"Yes." Vivien touched the cat's head. Smoke sizzled from between her fingers.

The cat's eyes opened and it started to yowl in pain.

"What?" Bridget picked the cat up gingerly, afraid of making the situation worse. It was still badly hurt, but at least it was alive. "Viv-?"

Their friend had collapsed in the middle of the bike lane.

Gertie was frozen in place. What had Vivien just done?

"Gertie?" Bridget asked, looking up at her sister.

"It's overexertion," Gertie said, finally finding her voice. She kneeled and lifted the much taller girl up, heaving her arm over her shoulder. "She'll be fine after a rest."

Bridget took the cat back to the car and cuddled the pained creature in her lap as Gertie all but dragged Vivien along behind. It groaned and hissed but allowed Bridget to fuss over it.

"Let's get the cat to Faye," Bridget said, her jaw locked in determination. "She'll be able to heal him."

Gertie buckled Vivien into the back seat and got in the driver's chair. She turned the car back on and clicked the magical driver button. It waited for instructions.

"We need to get back to Flories Boarding School," she told it. "It's an emergency."

The car turned its blinker on and pulled out into the road, tires wailing. It made it to the left lane by the next light and executed a speedy, but perfectly safe, U-turn.

Vivien stirred at the motion and opened her eyes.

"I'm starving," she mumbled, reaching into her backpack. She had some freshly baked cornbread in a tupperware container and started tearing into it. The smell wafted through the car, making Bridget's mouth water.

"Of course you are," Gertie scolded. "You nearly killed yourself."

"No I didn't, I just haven't done much spirit work lately," Vivien said.

"And never with *real* spirits," Gertie retorted. "What were you thinking, stitching the cat's spirit back into it's body? You could have really hurt yourself."

Vivien glared. "I'm fine, aren't I?"

The cat yowled, annoyed at the arguing.

"Will you two be quiet?" Bridget said. The car pulled up next to the school, its hazards on.

"Go park," Vivien told it once they had all unloaded. The car drove away, legally allowed to control itself while empty inside a parking lot.

The three rushed to Faye Nessing's room. In the few weeks she had been at Flories, she had become known as a prodigy when it came to healing animals.

They banged on the door and Faye answered, her roommates looking annoyed behind her at being woken so early.

"What?" she snapped. She saw the cat in Bridget's arms and gasped. "Hi there," she said, crooning now. She checked his collar. "Erwin. Hi Erwin, what happened to you?"

The cat yowled, sounding almost like speech.

Faye's mouth dropped open. "They hit you with a *car*?"

Bridget had known that one of the Nessing girl's necklaces allowed her to speak to dogs. It seemed she had another that

71

worked on cats.

"It was an accident," Bridget mumbled, wiping away the tears that formed again. "Can you tell him I'm sorry?"

Faye pulled supplies down from her little dorm closet, mumbling about *idiot humans*, while Bridget watched on forlornly.

Nervously, Faye's roommates picked up their purses and backpacks and shuffled out, leaving the healer to her business. They had been on the wrong end of distracting Faye from her work enough in her limited time at Flories, and weren't excited for another lecture.

Vivien, meanwhile, was sitting against the wall outside the open door, chewing absentmindedly on her cornbread and deep in thought.

Gertie sat next to her. "You want to talk about it?" she asked, trying to be gentle.

Vivien took a deep breath and sighed. "What I did was beginning necromancy," she said. "And it was so easy. I didn't even think about it."

Gertie nodded.

Vivien shifted, letting her head rest on Gertie's shoulder. "I know that it's...so incredibly dangerous," Vivien said. "And...scary. And bad."

"It's not always bad," Gertie granted her. "It just...has a history of being used for bad things."

Vivien nodded, thinking of the wars against evil necromancers who had raised armies of the dead that she had been taught about in history classes. She took a deep breath. "The thing is...I just find spirit magic *fascinating*, you know? Even when it comes to necromancy."

"Yeah, I do." Gertie smiled. "I just don't feel the same way."

"I mean, I don't want to spend *all* my time raising the dead," Vivien assured her. "There's lots of other magic we can still do." Vivien offered Gertie a piece of the cornbread. Gertie took a bite. Vivien made the most tempting baked goods.

"Hand me that brush?" Faye asked Bridget, and Gertie turned to watch.

Bridget reached for one from a cup on Faye's desk.

"No."

Bridget pointed to another one.

"No."

Bridget reached for the last one in the cup.

Faye gestured impatiently. "No! The one with the blue bristles."

Vivien breathed in deep and let it out in a frustrated huff. "What do I do?"

Gertie tried to focus on their conversation again. "Hm?"

"About the...necromancy?"

Gertie thought about what she would do if there was something she really wanted to study, despite her misgivings about what Vivien wanted to learn. "Ask Headmistress Clearwater if she can arrange a class for next year," she said. "Or sign up for a summer course at one of the colleges in the city. Or an online class. Or-"

"Okay, I get it." Vivien smiled.

Gertie hesitated, staring down at the bread in her hand.

Vivien nudged her with her arm. "Hey, I'll be ok. I won't go skipping rules and regulations. I'll do it right this time."

Gertie tried to clamp down on the nerves bubbling in her chest at the thought of everything that could go wrong for Vivien if she went down this path. "Yeah, you will."

"Okay, it took everything I've got, but he's good as new," Faye said, handing Erwin back to Bridget. "You owe me one favor."

"I can pay in your favorite baked good," Vivien said as she and Gertie stood.

Faye scoffed. "I don't think you understand how much energy and material this-"

Vivien offered her a piece of the cornbread.

Faye picked it up, sniffed it, and took a bite. Her eyes opened wide. Gertie and Bridget knew Vivien's baking; it was likely the best cornbread Faye had ever eaten.

"Yeah, okay, alright." Faye nodded. "Two dozen apricot turnovers sound fair?"

Vivien nodded. "Expect them next weekend."

The girls found Vivien's car again, parked in the back of the lot. Erwin purred in Bridget's arms, having apparently forgiven her for almost killing him. Faye must have passed along a sufficiently persuasive apology after all.

Gertie read the address from Erwin's collar to the car, and it rumbled to life, taking them to a small house near the campus.

They rang the doorbell and waited nervously.

A pleasant-looking woman answered the door.

"Erwin!" she said, accepting the cat without a word from the girls. "Where did you get off to?"

The cat began yowling to her in the same way he had spoken to Faye. Bridget bit her lip from her nerves, trying to figure out the excuse she would give to Erwin's owner as the cat ratted her out.

"Oh, you little fluffer, let's get you inside," the woman said, placing the cat on the floor. He sniffed and stalked off into the house. His owner turned back to the girls. "Thank you for bringing him back. Did you find him on campus? He loves the flowers there."

"Yes," Bridget said, letting out a sigh of relief. "Erwin sure does love flowers."

Vivien offered the tupperware to the woman. "Cornbread?"

Gertie and Bridget take a test

"Hey, Ernest," Charlie Nessing said, gesturing for Ernest to join him and his brother Peter on the side of the classroom as everyone packed up to leave the latest Magic Club meeting.

"Yeah?" Ernest perked up and hurried to put away his things. He and the Nessing brothers had developed a shallow friendship within the Magic Club, but asking to talk to him after? That was new territory.

Charlie peered over at Mr. Jerson, the Magic Club faculty advisor. He wasn't paying attention, but even so, Charlie tilted his head to indicate that they should leave the room.

Ernest followed Charlie and Peter down the hall, and Gertie, Bridget, and Vivien stopped to wait, watching the three boys.

Charlie took a deep breath. "I was hoping you could help us with something."

Ernest tried to show concern, instead of delight at being asked. "Help you with what?"

Charlie jolted at Ernest's volume. At the word 'help', Gertie,

Bridget and Vivien edged closer.

"The Flories School Exit Exam is coming up," Charlie said, keeping his voice low. "Headmistress Clearwater told Peter that if he doesn't pass it, he'll be held back from graduating and will have to take summer school."

Peter nodded grimly, standing at his brother's shoulder.

"Really? You've only been here a few weeks." Ernest said.

Charlie nodded. "I'm aware," he said bitterly.

"That sucks," Ernest said.

"That can't be fair," Gertie interjected, coming up behind Ernest. Vivien and Bridget followed her. "Did your parents try calling the headmistress?"

Charlie frowned, not making eye contact. "We talked to them. They said he should 'study hard'."

"I'm sorry," Gertie said.

"I've already been admitted to Wespire U. If I don't pass, they might..." Peter let his head hang. "I'm not the best test taker. Especially with that sort of threat hanging over me."

"It's such a stupid test," Ernest grumbled. "I failed the last two years and have to take it again. I'll probably end up in summer school too."

"Wow, I didn't know it was that bad," Gertie said, looking worriedly at Bridget. "This is our first year at Flories, so we have to take it."

"At least you'll have more chances," Ernest said.

Vivien, who had taken the F-SEE her sophomore year and hadn't had much of a problem passing her first attempt, bit her bottom lip and kept silent.

"I mean," Ernest continued. "It's just not fair. If I pass my classes, I should be able to graduate, right? Why should I have to keep taking the test until I scrape by?"

"Well," Charlie said, pushing his thick-rimmed glasses up his nose. "What if we knew we were going to do well this time?"

Faye Nessing, Peter and Charlie's younger sister, suddenly ran out of the classroom and pushed her way into the circle.

"I can hear what you're saying in there," she muttered. "Mr. Jerson was on the phone, but he's coming now so-"

"I mean," Peter suddenly said, seeing over Faye's head that Mr. Jerson had entered the hallway. "If they kept the pool any colder during practice, my fingers would fall off. And that wouldn't heal so easy, you know?"

"Yeah, you'd need an even more expensive charm to heal something like that," Charlie said, good naturedly nudging his brother.

Peter laughed and played with the necklace around his neck. Bridget had noticed it had an enchantment on it; a healing spell would explain why they had seen him mend so quickly after getting in a fight.

"Have a good night, you guys," Mr. Jerson said, waving as he headed in the opposite direction.

"You too!" Charlie replied with a grin. As soon as Mr. Jerson was gone, Charlie lowered his voice considerably. "Ok, so-"

"I don't have to take the test until next year, and I have some homework and healing to do," Faye interrupted. "If you get caught, make sure to mention I wasn't involved."

As the youngest Nessing sibling stalked off, Gertie and Bridget turned back to Charlie.

"Get caught?" Gertie repeated.

"What is she talking about?" Bridget asked.

"Headmistress Clearwater has the test booklets and the answer keys in her office," Charlie explained, looking at Ernest. "After the way you handled the lock on that trick box, I was thinking you wouldn't have any trouble getting us in. We grab a booklet and an answer key and we're golden!"

Charlie and Peter nodded at Ernest, their expressions pleading. Ernest took a deep breath. "Well..."

"I don't think that's a good idea," Gertie said, putting a hand on Ernest's shoulder.

He didn't move when she pulled. "Ernest, you're not a cheater-" she started.

"Neither are we!" Charlie protested. "But think about what'll happen otherwise!"

"What will the headlines say?" Peter asked. "'Mayoral candidate Felix Nessing's children fail out of school'?"

"I mean, by that logic," Gertie said. "Can you imagine the same headline if you get caught *stealing*?"

"Oh come on," Peter scoffed. "Like you've never used magic to pull one over on non-practitioners."

Gertie and Bridget couldn't argue with that.

"Besides, do you really want to stay here any longer than you have to?" Charlie directed this at Ernest. "We can't do it without you."

"I think we're just going to go grab some dinner," Vivien said sternly.

Gertie tried pulling Ernest away again.

"I'm in," he said, yanking his arm away from Gertie. He wouldn't meet their gaze as they stared in disbelief. "I'll just grab my ukulele from my dorm. My magic will be more powerful that way."

The Nessing brothers and Ernest walked towards the dorms, talking about the extent of Ernest's musical magical gifts. Bridget, Gertie and Vivien watched them go.

"Pastapolis?" Bridget suggested.

"Yeah," Gertie said, trying to push the feeling of betrayal down. "I'm starving."

✿ ✿ ✿

The next morning, on their way to breakfast, Gertie, Bridget and Vivien took a detour to Lonaickey Hall, the administrative building on campus. Gertie had a form that needed the Headmistress' signature in order for her to to receive credit from an online course towards her enchanting apprenticeship license. Technically, the Headmistress' administrative assistant, Toby, didn't work on the weekend. But he was behind on paperwork and had told her he would be in the office and that Gertie could stop by.

"Plus," Bridget had said, "We can see if the Nessings left any evidence."

The building sure looked empty, despite the front door being unlocked.

The three girls passed the Headmistress' office in order to go to the receptionist's desk.

"I don't see anything," Gertie said, glancing around the

surrounding hallway.

"Hey! Gertie! Is that you?" came a whisper.

Gertie paused, sharing a glance with Bridget. "Ernest?"

"Yeah!"

"Where are you?" Bridget hissed.

"Headmistress' office!" came the anxious reply.

The three girls descended on the hallway door with "Headmistress Clearwater" printed in gold lettering on it.

"I thought you'd be long gone with the answers by now," Gertie hissed back.

"We couldn't!"

The door was ajar, and Bridget pulled it all the way open.

"Well, look at that," Bridget said smugly. It was too good.

They were all trapped.

Ernest was covered in large, sticky spiderwebs, stuck against the very door Bridget had pulled open.

Peter was rolled up in the Headmistress' dusty old rug, looking like a baby that had been thoroughly swaddled.

Charlie had managed to avoid both traps. He had failed, however, to notice that the cabinet was also enchanted, and it had sprayed him with a sleeping potion. He now snoozed with his face pressed against a half-open drawer, his glasses on the floor.

"Oh, did we forget to tell you that Headmistress Clearwater actually believes in magical security?" Gertie said. "Whoops."

"Look, Gertie. We've been here all night," Ernest said.

"We didn't even take the answers," Peter added.

"Just get us out of here so we can go home!" Ernest pleaded.

Charlie let out a rather loud snore.

"I don't know," Gertie said. "You being stuck here the rest of the weekend might be just what you need to realize that-"

"Oh, come on, Gertie." Vivien good-naturedly pushed past her to investigate the webbing encasing Ernest. "It looks like a classic Spicron hunting enchantment. Just look up the release spell."

Gertie huffed, but pulled out her phone.

"And that's just an enchanted rug," Vivien said. She fingered a thread pulling away from Peter's trap. "Bridget, do you have any-?"

Bridget pulled a utility knife from her bag and opened the scissor attachment.

Vivien cut the thread, and the charm on the rug released, allowing Peter to wriggle himself free.

"You owe me two hours of sitting and charging my keychains," Gertie informed Ernest as she drew on her stored power. She spoke the magic words that the online encyclopedia article said would release a Spicron enchantment.

The webbing melted away, leaving a large amount of white goop on the Headmistress' carpets.

"That's not going to be easy to clean up," Peter said as he stood and stretched. His forehead was badly bruised from when he hit the floor, but faded as Bridget watched the magic on his necklace spark. He reached down and picked up his younger brother, hoisting him over his shoulder, and hung his glasses from his shirt collar. "Come on. I'm sure Faye can figure out what happened to him."

The sound of the building's front door opening as they left the Headmistress' office made them all freeze.

"Back door!" Bridget hissed.

Vivien twisted the lock on the inside of the doorknob and pushed the Headmistress' door closed. Everyone ran through the hallway, going for the back door that exited into the school's parking lot.

Except Gertie, who walked in the opposite direction.

"Good morning, Toby," Gertie said, as she entered Lonaickey's lobby from the side hallway. Toby, Headmistress Clearwater's assistant, smiled in greeting.

"Got the form?"

"Right here." Gertie pulled the envelope from her back pocket.

"Great. I'll have Abigail sign it first thing on Monday and I'll send it in for you. Have a great weekend!"

"You too!" Gertie hesitated. "I mean, even if you're working, I'm sure-"

"I know what you meant." Toby smiled and headed to the Headmistress' office.

Gertie made it out of the front door before she heard the shouting.

"I've told her a thousand times this would happen!" Toby groaned, seeing the mess that the Spicron trap had left. "What's wrong with cameras? Why all this magical nonsense? There's nothing even *here*! A mouse probably set it off!"

Bridget, Vivien, Ernest, and Peter, carrying Charlie, joined Gertie as she walked away.

"I hope you've learned your lesson," Gertie said.

"Of course we have," Peter assured her.

Ernest nodded, looking guilty that he had even attempted to

cheat.

Vivien smiled. "Good."

❖ ❖ ❖

A week later the F-SEE grades were posted. All the students who had taken the test crowded around the bulletin board, trying to see if they passed, and where they had ranked among other students.

Gertie and Bridget were relieved to see that they both had P's next to their names. Bridget was even high up on the list.

Then they saw who was at the top.

Ernest and the Nessing brothers were hanging out across the hallway by the water fountain, watching the crowd with amusement without even glancing at the list. Why would they? They knew what they got.

Gertie and Bridget strode over furiously, ready to let loose a verbal lashing. Ernest, at least, had the decency to look ashamed.

Before the sisters could start, Charlie managed to take all the wind out of their sails.

"Thanks for your help," he said with a grin.

Gertie gets her license

Gertie looked up at the entrance to the Skyline stadium. Normally, when she was in the sports arena of the magical city above the clouds, it was to see a game of basketball with virtually no limits on magic, or a gladiator battle (with safety spells implemented and a healer present), or a dragon presentation.

This time, all the bleachers had been pushed back into the walls, and the floor was lined with little sound-proof cubicles. Inside each was a mini kitchen set up via magic, and a proctor waiting for their examinee.

It was the day of the Enchantment Apprenticeship License Exam.

The exam was an international event, spanning across more than seventy locations throughout the twenty countries that recognized the exam as a fitting qualification for an apprenticeship. All over the world, hopefuls were taking the test that Gertie was about to embark on.

Gertie checked herself in for the afternoon test block she had signed up for. It was right after the lunch break in the test schedule - there was no way she was risking the license she'd been working towards for the last two years on a cranky proctor who was daydreaming of macaroni and cheese.

The man at the sign-in table took her cellphone and backpack to be locked away and gave her her assigned cubicle number. Gertie thanked him, took a deep breath, and descended the stairs to find her testing spot.

She had stored plenty of power in her keychain accessories, practiced her planned enchantment hundreds of times, and wore her lucky cloche hat. It wasn't magical - that wasn't allowed in exams - but Gertie always did well on tests when she wore it. She was ready, she told herself. She would be fine.

"Miss Mallon?" asked the woman standing in her assigned cubicle with a clipboard.

Gertie nodded.

"I'm going to scan you for magical objects." She held up a wand to do so.

"I have my keychains, for power, since I'm not a witch," Gertie said, pulling them out for the proctor to see. She had written this on her application, so it wasn't a surprise.

"Set them down there." The proctor nodded to the table where a whole slew of potion ingredients sat.

Gertie did so.

The proctor took her wand and did a quick scan from the floor, over Gertie's left shoulder, head, right shoulder, and back to the ground.

She then waved the wand over Gertie's keychains, testing them for any enchantments as well.

"Looks good. Let's get started."

Gertie picked up her keychains again and put them back into her pocket.

Her proctor read from a clipboard. "Your self-selected enchantment is the Floating Bag. We have provided you with everything you will need. You have an hour and a half to complete your enchantment. Begin."

Gertie went straight to the stack of equipment in the corner. She chose a cast iron cauldron that was the same size she'd practiced with in her dorm room. She put it on the stove and cranked the heat to medium.

A bottle of cloud extract was sitting, tall and with a no-drip spout, on the back corner of the table laden with ingredients. Gertie picked it up and coated the bottom of her cauldron with the wispy white gel. Next, she measured out the moonflower pollen, according to the recipe she had memorized, and put it in the extract to sizzle.

While that was going, she started chopping, skinning, and grinding everything she needed. Gertie had found the electric mixer and was whipping up cream from winged cows when disaster struck.

The pollen in the cauldron started popping.

Gertie dropped the bowl of whipped cream onto the table and stared at the pollen that was jumping out of the cauldron. What was going on? She put a splatter screen over the top of the cauldron to keep the pollen from escaping, and picked up the jar she had measured from.

She felt her ears roaring as she stared at it blankly.

Moonflower pollen, aged ten years, the label read. *Ten years*.

She had been practicing with five.

The pollen popped so high the splatter guard jumped before settling back.

She glanced up. The proctor was taking notes, frowning.

Gertie grit her teeth until her head hurt. She could fix this. She didn't know much about creating new spells, so she wouldn't be able to change the actual incantation to suit this new recipe. But maybe she could add something that would counteract the effects of the extra aging.

The test had provided her with more ingredients than she needed, to throw her off in case she hadn't memorized the right recipe. Maybe something they had given her would actually help.

Gertie glanced over the plethora of ingredients. Snake venom, no. Pie crust, what would that even-? Rice? Yes! Plain old rice! A common ingredient in underwater potions, it normally would do the exact opposite of what Gertie's enchantment needed.

But normally, she would have used the right pollen.

Carefully, after triple-checking the label, Gertie measured out the proper amount of rice to counteract the aging of the pollen and poured it into the pot.

She turned up the heat and added the rest of the ingredients.

Gertie left her potion to boil and turned to chop up the last item - lavender.

After that was done, there was nothing to do but wait. Well, wait and clean up the space. That was what the provided sink was for, after all.

Once the chopping boards, bowls, knives, and peeler were all clean, the timer rang.

The next step was to soak the bag that she was enchanting in the potion.

But before she did that, Gertie sprinkled the lavender into the mix. The aroma of the herb filled the cubicle, chasing away the odd scent of burnt pollen and silkworm saliva. It wasn't strictly necessary, but Gertie preferred the smell of her enchantments to not render the objects unusable.

Gertie killed the heat on the stove and dropped her bag in.

She stirred it into the potion with a wooden spoon, drawing power from her keychains as she spoke her spell clearly, since the proctor would grade on pronunciation.

The potion glowed a clear and brilliant green. Perfect.

Gertie used the spoon to fish the bag out of the potion.

There was one last step. Gertie took a deep breath. She used this specific spell every morning when she dried her hair after getting out of the shower. There was nothing to be nervous about, and yet her heart beat so rapidly she thought it would stall.

"Dry," she commanded in the magical language of Gnaang, flicking the bag and sending the potion flying into the sink, coating it green.

Gertie quickly set the nozzle to rinse the basin, and then held out the dry cloth bag for the proctor to inspect.

The proctor looked at her watch.

"Twenty-six minutes early," she said, taking note. "But you didn't wait for it to dry naturally-"

"I've tried letting it, like the recipe says," Gertie quickly said. "I can just barely do it under the time limit. But I *had* to try using the drying spell, just to see, and it works! The bag still works."

The proctor looked over her glasses at Gertie. "And *why* does it work?"

Gertie took a deep breath to keep herself from rambling. "Because the spell imbues the power from the potion into the bag itself, in this case," Gertie said. "If the potion coating the bag was necessary for peak performance, it would *have* to be air dried."

"Correct." The proctor wrote down some notes. "Now, let's see if it works. I noticed your mistake with the pollen, but the rice was clever. It should have helped."

The proctor took the bag and said, "Float," in Gnaang, releasing the bag in midair. It hung there, as if it had been placed on a table.

The proctor took a step to the left and the bag followed. To the right, the same thing. She started walking away, and the bag floated after her.

The proctor nodded thoughtfully, taking down notes. "You still didn't follow the recipe, I'm afraid," she said.

Gertie's heart fell. Surely her final score would be impacted for not following the exact steps in the approved recipe.

"We both normally get a fifteen minute break before the next part of the test. However, that would be at the end of the hour and a half, which there is still twenty minutes of. Would you like to wait a full thirty minutes or...?"

"I don't think I can wait that long," Gertie admitted, anxious to get on with the next part of the test.

The proctor smiled. "Fifteen minutes then."

Gertie found the bathroom. Her hands shook as she washed them.

One down, one to go.

She returned to her cubicle and sipped water until the proctor returned.

"Alright. Your first enchantment you were able to practice. This one, you have not. We've given you all new ingredients." The proctor gestured to the table. There was no over-aged pollen in sight. "Follow the instructions, use your intuition, and you will hopefully be fine. You have one hour. Good luck."

She handed Gertie a piece of paper.

Glowing Orchid Encased in Glass, was the recipe title. Sure enough, a beautiful purple orchid sat in a pot in the corner of the mini kitchen's counter.

Not a very creative recipe name, Gertie thought.

Then she glanced down at the *three* separate sections of the recipe.

"Balls," Gertie muttered, and grabbed three separate cauldrons from the corner. All three went on the heat.

She only had an hour and a half to make three different potions? It was madness.

Even more ridiculous was that they didn't give her the whole recipe. They gave her bits and pieces, and she needed to rely on her potion know-how to complete the recipe.

The first thing under the title was *Step 1: Make a coolant*, with a list of ingredients and their measurements.

Gertie remembered the word coolant. She had spent a lot of her time watching various potions videos online to try to prepare.

Coolants are the easiest potions in the world! an online potion maker had proclaimed. *You just put all your ingredients in the pot, put the lid on, and boil it for thirty minutes until everything's combined. Then you shove it in the fridge to cool it down and it's ready!*

Gertie measured out all of the coolant's ingredients and threw them in the cauldron on the back burner of the stove and put the lid on. She set a timer for thirty minutes, and let it do its own thing.

Step 2: Combine the following ingredients to make the clear syrup base for the luminance potion.

This was the potion that would make the orchid glow. Gertie racked her brain - potions that emitted light could be tricky. There were lots of variations, but all needed to be done at a precise temperature to determine what color it would be. Since the recipe specified *clear*, it meant the lowest of the available temperatures.

Just remember the eight eights, she remembered her potions textbook saying on the subject of potion color. *Eighty-eight for black, seventy-eight for purple, sixty-eight for blue, fifty-eight green, forty-eight for for yellow, thirty-eight for orange, twenty-eight for red, eighteen for clear.*

Gertie took a deep breath and grinned in relief.

She measured tiny crystals of lightning salt into a cup to pour into the final cauldron and an equal amount of starfruit seeds. She added the required teaspoon of moonshade - a sticky golden syrup - and filled the rest of the cauldron with water.

She stirred it diligently, checking on the nearby coolant with eyes only. She had to keep the glowing potion constantly moving, while checking the temperature on a thermometer and adjusting the stove accordingly to keep it at eighteen degrees.

Finally, the potion for the glow started to thicken and form sparking bubbles.

"Yes!" Gertie fist pumped.

Step 3: When the syrup has begun to bubble, let it boil on the stove for fifteen minutes.

Gertie set a timer for fifteen minutes, and sat down for a moment to catch her breath and read ahead in the recipe.

The fourth step was about adding something to the luminance potion, so Gertie skipped over it.

Step 5: Choose the proper incantation to melt the glass.

Choose the proper...?

Gertie turned the recipe sheet over. On the opposite side was a list of spells. At least they were all in Laux, a language she knew. Of course, this was not a coincidence since she had provided the accredited board with a list of her capabilities when applying to take the test.

Gertie took a deep breath and began translating the spells to the best of her ability. Three she ruled out of being a part of this enchantment altogether - they mentioned eggs and things that weren't on the ingredients table. One she discovered, upon translating, was for when she had finished brewing the luminance potion. She circled that one for later.

There were three that mentioned glass. One was clearly the end of the enchantment, as it meant the equivalent of "Halt." The two others were trickier. They were very similar, longer spells, both dealing with the glass. One did have the word for "liquid" in it, so she put a star next to it in the hopes that she was right.

Both timers rang that their potions were ready and Gertie re-

read step four.

Step 4: Once the syrup's bubbles have begun to stack, add one fourth teaspoon of star spider venom and let the potion rest for four minutes.

Gertie stared at the instruction. Venoms were pesky things, very reactive. Usually recipes mentioned not moving the pot, putting on a lid, and using a timer to measure exactly the amount of time it needed to sit.

Gertie checked the clock to see how much time she had left. Twenty minutes. Great.

She returned to the luminance potion. It had boiled so much, it looked like an ambitious bubble bath.

"Bubbles stacking on themselves, check," Gertie said.

She had no choice but to listen to her intuition, even if it was wrong. She added the final ingredient - the venom of a star spider - and clamped the cauldron's lid down. She set a timer for four minutes exactly and one for three minutes and fifteen seconds to remind her to come back, and turned her attention to the shards of glass she had been provided with. She needed to magically melt them.

Gertie poured them into the last cauldron she had put to heat on the stove. She spoke the enchantment she had chosen over the glass, and watched as they melted instantly.

"Awesome!" Gertie triumphantly slipped on cauldron mitts, took the mix off the stove and set it next to the provided mold for the final sculpture.

The mold itself was a sphere with a flat bottom, so that the eventual decoration could stand upright. It was made of magically imbued silicone, so it would be resistant to the heat of the glass.

Suddenly the smell of smoke filled the air. Gertie stopped and looked over at the stove.

No, Gertie thought. *No no no no no.*

The coolant.

She had completely forgotten to take it off the stove and put it in the freezer.

Gertie ran to the stove and looked in the pot. It was crusted black. Nothing was salvageable. She put the entire thing into the sink and ran cold water over it, trying to stop the smoke at the very least.

Gertie stared at the running water, trying to figure a way out. What was she going to do? There was no way she could make a whole new potion. It needed time, not only to combine but to cool. She felt like she had been turned to stone, her heart trying to beat out of her chest.

The three minute and fifteen second timer for the luminance potion rang, and Gertie took a deep breath. She wasn't going down without a fight.

The proctor made a note, but Gertie didn't have time to think about her opinion.

Step 6: Remove the luminance potion from the heat and cast the proper incantation that will stabilize it for use.

When the four minute timer rang, Gertie pulled the cauldron off the stove, opened the lid, and spoke the spell she'd circled from the list, the one she hoped would render it stable.

The potion started glowing a solid white color, like she had trapped a star in her cauldron.

Gertie let out a deep breath. That was a very good sign.

She assembled the leftovers of her prepared ingredients that she had made into the first coolant potion. There wasn't enough to make a whole potion, so a third of the original recipe's portion would have to do.

She stirred the ingredients together on the stove, trying to force everything to melt as quickly as possible in lieu of it boiling together. When it finally became a thin, watery potion, she took it off the heat and poured it into a metal bowl to suck the heat away. She put the bowl into the freezer, and turned back to deal with the rest of the recipe.

"Five minutes," the proctor said, checking her timer, a nervous edge to her voice.

Gertie balled her hands into fists, digging her nails into her palms. Fine.

She opened the freezer and put her hands on the bowl. She could still feel the heat emanating from the potion.

"Chill," she said in Laux, feeling the power drain from her keychains and flow through her hands. The temperature in the bowl went down. But it wasn't cool enough.

"Chill," she said again, gritting her teeth as she started to feel dizzy from using magic so quickly twice in a row.

Not enough.

"Chill!" she shouted, and the heat vanished from under her hands, nearly numbing them.

She took the bowl out and placed it next to the luminance potion, trying not to lose her balance. The coolant didn't even slosh, it had thickened so much from the cold.

Gertie pulled over the terracotta pot that the orchid was in. She snipped its stem so that it was short enough to fit inside the mold and, taking a deep breath, dipped the flower into the luminance potion.

As the instructions read, she immediately pulled it out and shoved it into the coolant, hissing as steam flew out from around her hand. Could that be a good thing?

She had to spin the stem around to coat the flower petals completely. Since she'd made only a third of the proper amount, what was left barely covered the bottom of the bowl.

Gertie lifted the orchid free. It glowed with the pure brilliance of a perfectly brewed luminance potion, shifting between the various purples, whites and yellows of the flower that were picked up by the potion.

The proctor smiled and wrote on her clipboard.

Gertie would have danced in place, but she didn't have time.

She took the glass mixture, still melted and waiting thanks to the spell, and poured a bit of it into the mold, so the orchid would be floating in the middle. She placed the orchid delicately, and managed to pour the rest of the glass in around it. At the last minute, she remembered the final incantation she had singled out - this one mentioning "not wilting". The heat from the glass seemed to dissipate, leaving the orchid beautifully fresh.

Gertie put down the heavy cauldron and took a moment to pant.

"And halt," she said in Laux, completing the enchantment.

The glass hardened instantly.

And the proctor's timer beeped.

Gertie heart caught in her throat. She hadn't turned out the sculpture. It wasn't done. She hadn't finished.

"Take it out of the mold," the proctor said.

Gertie looked over at her, dumbfounded.

"I'll mark you off a point for not finishing it in the time. But turn it out. I'm going to grade it."

Gertie took the quite heavy mold and turned it over. The glass held steady.

She pulled the mold free, peeling it away from the glass. And there it was. Her little "glowing orchid encased in glass."

It was quite impressive, she had to say. Beautiful even. A good way to end her exam, even if she had failed.

The proctor took a deep breath, as if to calm herself from the excitement of Gertie's scramble to finish. She hovered around the table, looking at the sculpture from every angle. She pulled a small camera out of her pocket, took a picture of the top of her clipboard and one of the sculpture.

Gertie waited, shifting awkwardly in place. Her head cleared a bit, despite how she had drained herself by spending so much magic.

The proctor checked over her clipboard, wrote some notes, and finally said, "Very good, Miss Mallon. If you just go back to the area you found the sign-in desk, there will also be a sign-out desk. There, they will take your picture and you will receive your license. Your sculpture will be mailed to your registered address in a week's time. If you have any other questions or concerns-"

"I passed?" Gertie clarified, not believing her ears.

"Yes," the proctor said. "Of course."

Gertie thanked her and walked in a daze to the sign-out table. She managed a smile for the photo, and received a printed license within minutes.

Holding it in her hands, reading the words, *Apprentice Enchanter,* under her name, suddenly made it real.

She whooped, holding the license triumphantly in the air.

Upon receiving her backpack and cell phone, she immediately dialed Bridget. "I did it!" Gertie shouted. She heard different voices cheering from the other side.

"We're all in your room," Bridget said, a laugh in her voice. "We have cake and sodas. Get back down here!"

"Awesome!" Gertie said. "I'm on my way!"

She dialed one more number as she headed out of the stadium.

"Demetrius' Enchanted Hat Emporium, Demetrius speaking," came a bored voice from the other end.

"D?" Gertie said excitedly.

He paused. "Gertie, tell me you have good news."

Gertie grinned so hard her face hurt. "I do."

To her surprise, Demetrius laughed in relief. "I knew you could do it!"

"Thanks," Gertie said, flattered, but itching to ask a very important question. "So, when can I start as your apprentice? I've been looking up different hat enchantments. I was thinking an expandable hat might be a good place to start. I know that top hats are generally the favored model, but to me that just makes it less incredible that you can fit all that stuff in. My choice would definitely be porkpie, or a-"

"Uh, Gertie, I have a customer."

"I don't believe you," Gertie said.

"Just go celebrate. We can talk about all this during your next shift."

"My *last* shift stacking boxes," Gertie shot back.

"Yeah." The pride was unmistakable in his voice. Demetrius hung up before he could embarrass himself any further.

As Gertie got in the elevator back down to Wespire, her ID was required. Normally, her magical passport filled this purpose.

Not this time.

Gertie dramatically held out her enchanter's license to the scanner.

Gertrude Mallon, Apprentice Enchanter.

Gertie and Bridget go on a field trip

Thanks to the success of the bake sale, largely driven by Vivien's school-famous cupcakes, the entirety of Flories Boarding School's Magic Club was going on a field trip.

At six am sharp on a Saturday morning, the twenty or so students filed onto the bright blue school bus. It pulled out of the parking lot, and the club began the three hour drive to the coast.

Gertie took her seat next to Bridget, with Vivien and Ernest taking the two in front of them.

"I can't believe how long this is going to take," Ernest said, pulling out his phone to decide what music to listen to.

Vivien rolled her eyes and sat up on her knees to look over the back of her seat and talk to Gertie and Bridget. "What do you think it's going to be like?" she asked. "I've never been out of the country before. This kind of counts, right?"

Bridget nodded. "I mean, we did have to bring passports."

Mr. Jerson, the Magic Club's faculty advisor, was talking with an unfamiliar man whose hair had been dyed a bright green. He nodded to Mr. Jerson, and stood at the front of the bus with a microphone attached to the bus PA system.

"Hello, everyone," he said. "My name is Will, and I'll be your tour guide on the way to and in the Mermaid city-state of Daallu."

Vivien's eyes widened and she sat back down to pay attention.

"Daallu, like all Mermaid cities, is on the ocean floor in international waters." Will grabbed onto the closest seat to steady himself as the bus jolted. "That means that even though Daallu is close enough to our fine country of Crescyth to be accessed by underwater tunnel, the government here in Crescyth has nothing to do with Daallu. Every Mermaid city-state has its own government, and we're very lucky that Daallu lets in human visitors. Not all coastside ones do, and for some of the deeper cities, you need all sorts of special visas, even for a day trip."

The bus came to a halt again, pitching the tour guide back, and Will sighed. "You know what? I'll tell you more when the traffic dies down."

He sat back in his seat and turned off the whining microphone.

"This is so exciting!" Vivien said, bouncing in her bus seat.

"Yeah!" Gertie agreed. "I've never seen an animoid before! I have so many questions!"

"It's possible you've met an animoid using a transformation spell," Charlie Nessing said matter-of-factly, standing to lean over the seat back and correct Gertie. "And you just didn't know. You shouldn't make assumptions."

"Was I talking to you?" Gertie snapped back, flushing. He was right.

"I'm just saying you shouldn't act like they're a zoo exhibit. It's rude."

"Who are you to call anyone rude, Charlie?" Vivien asked.

Charlie just glared and sat down again.

Bridget pulled out a deck of cards from her bag. "Want to play something?" she offered Gertie as a distraction.

Three hands of "Fox of Spades" later, Will stood up again.

"I have a list of things I'm supposed to remind you." He pulled a folded piece of paper from his pocket. "First, while the native Mermaid language is Mmeerruuk, they are much better at foreign language education in Daallu than most Mermaid cities, so you should be able to speak to everyone. They won't accept your paper money, so I hope everyone followed the advice of the email Mr. Jerson sent out and went to an exchange for occozh, the Mermaid currency, if you want to buy any trinkets. Lunch and dinner will be provided, and we've taken into consideration all of your listed diets."

Gertie grimaced. She was known to buy way too many souvenirs, so she and Bridget had opted to not get any occozh so they wouldn't be tempted.

"You'll be leaving your phones behind in the lockers, because I'm pretty sure you don't want them to break, but if anything's wrong, there are miraculously still payphones in Mermaid culture! Go to one and dial 753 for non-emergencies and 951 for emergencies. The Department of Outreach has been informed of our trip and will be able to contact me by emergency bubble. Hopefully you won't need to, but it's good to know just in case. This was all on the waiver you signed, and emergency numbers are listed on the payphones."

Will stepped toward the bus dashboard. "Now we're going to watch a quick film with more information for your visit. Before you get mad at me, it's required." He pressed a button and the TV screens throughout the bus flickered on.

"The city of Daallu has been around for centuries," a droning narrator said over stock footage of a beach. "Originally, a garrison against human invasion, and then a mere trading outpost, it is now one of the most prosperous Mer-cities that still allows outside visitors."

After fifteen minutes about the wonders of Daallu and Mermaid culture, Ernest put his earbuds in and Bridget pulled out a book.

"'Quick', yeah right," Faye Nessing muttered, pulling up a puzzle app on her phone.

Despite her best efforts, Gertie's eyes closed and she fell asleep. But Vivien held onto every word.

After what felt like an eternity, periodically interrupted by commentary from Will, the beach appeared. The bus pulled off the highway and into a small parking lot in a special "buses only" designated spot.

"And everybody off!" Will announced as the doors opened.

The students stepped off slowly, their legs stiff, taking in the sparkle of the beach and the brine scent in the air. Off to the right of the parking lot was a modern-looking wooden building with "Daallu Entrance" across the top. A glass hallway extended from the side, sloping into the water and beyond.

Will and Mr. Jerson led the way. They took care of all of the paperwork that needed to be done, handing over the stacks of forms that the students had filled out to the attendant at the front desk. The students milled around in the meantime, looking at the photographs of the city on the walls.

"The buildings are all round," Gertie remarked, looking at the cityscape.

"Probably better physics," Bridget said.

Vivien read the placard in the middle of the pictures.

"Wow, they use enchanted sand as their building material," Vivien murmured. A series of the pictures showed the process - using glowing blue runes to melt down sand into gray blocks, stacking them together in the proper formation, and then using white hot magic to fuse them together. "Imagine if everyone in our society had the capacity to use magic like that all the time."

"All right, we have two things for each of you," Will announced. He held out two plastic boxes. In one was a bunch of normal-looking orange inhalers. In the other, what looked like small, round clothespins.

"The first is the Ambifion inhaler," Will explained. "You take a puff and hold your breath for ten seconds. Then you do it again. It will grant you the ability to breathe underwater for two hours. When you start to cough orange, you'll need to do the whole process over, or you won't be able to breathe underwater anymore. That would, obviously, be very bad." Will waited for the severity of that possibility to set in, then continued. "Wait until you're in the entrance chambers to breathe it in for the first time, so you get as much underwater time as possible.

"The second is the waterproof clip. You get one for you, and one for your backpack or purse or what-have-you if you want to bring it. It will make your skin, hair, clothes, glasses, etcetera waterproof. We cannot guarantee it will fully work on cell phones, earbuds, tablets, laptops, non-magic cameras, calculators, or anything electronic. You will leave those behind in the lockers in the entrance chambers. You've all signed a form indicating you understand this."

"Everyone take what you need," Mr. Jerson said, and the students rushed forward.

Gertie put her inhaler in her pocket and affixed her waterproof clip to her belt. Bridget had a clip on her bag strap and one on the edge of her sleeve, and stuffed her inhaler in her bag.

"One more thing!" Mr. Jerson pulled a stack of papers and a bundle of pens from his satchel. "For fun, Will and I wrote up this little scavenger hunt. I waterproofed the paper and pens, don't worry. You'll just have to answer questions about places in the city that you can learn if you explore and ask questions. If you answer them all correctly by the time we get back on the bus, you get a Daallu postcard."

Peter raised his hand. "Can we work in groups?"

"Sure, why not? Groups of four. Everyone needs to fill out a sheet though, and write who you worked with on the top."

Bridget and Gertie took their scavenger hunt sheets and read them over.

"This could be cool," Bridget said.

Gertie grinned in excitement. "I want a free souvenir! Let's do it!"

"Bet we finish it before your group," Charlie said challengingly, motioning to his two siblings.

"You're on!" Gertie replied.

Mr. Jerson started through thick wooden doors that had been propped open and into the hallway to the ocean. As each student filed through behind him, they stopped and showed their passports to the security guards on either side, who checked them off a list. Gertie, Bridget, Ernest, and the Nessings had all qualified for entry much easier than their peers due to their standing in the practitioning community, and held up their magical passport cards without needing to wait in line.

They walked down the hall with the rest of the club lagging behind. While the tunnel started on the beach, giving a view of the sand and waves, it soon descended into the depths of the ocean. Gertie and Bridget stared out through the glass, admiring the various fish that milled in and out of the waving forests of seaweed and kelp.

"Give me some room, kids!" Will said, scooting around them to lead.

Charlie and Ernest frowned at being called "kids".

"This hallway was built forty-seven years ago, as a way to regulate entrances to the city for trade," Will explained. "Before then, anyone could take an Ambifion potion - though, back then you also would have had to drink them and that's much more of a shock to your body - and sink into the water and try to get into the city. 'Try' being the operative word. Mermaids were, and are, very protective of their land."

They took escalators down a particularly steep drop, and soon there wasn't much to see in the dim, murky water. Occasionally a large fish would approach the hall, made visible by the interior lights, and the students would jump before it vanished again.

Eventually, the club reached the end of the hallway. There was a line of metal doors, each with a green light above it signaling they could enter.

"Your teacher will go in first, and then you all can follow him and meet up on the other side." Will instructed. "Put everything you're not bringing into the lockers. They're water proof. Breathe in your potion last so you don't accidentally lock it away. Then press the big red button on the outside door."

Mr. Jerson stepped forward, opening one of the doors. The light above it changed to yellow as he prepped. It took a few minutes, but it eventually flipped back to green.

"Okay, all of you, one by one, into the chambers."

Gertie and Bridget went into separate rooms. The left wall of Gertie's chamber was entirely composed of lockers with keypads. As she stepped in, Gertie saw the locker that had been filled by the student preceding her slide backwards into the wall, and was quickly replaced by another. Gertie put her phone, earbuds, and keys (just in case) into the locker she chose, closed it, and typed in a code she often used for such things. The keypad was quickly replaced with a camera that snapped a picture of her face.

In Bridget's chamber, she blinked away the flash, having opted to just put her entire bag into the locker at the last minute, minus the scavenger hunt sheet and her inhaler.

There was a lit sign above the exit door that said, "Please take your Ambifion potion." Bridget held the inhaler to her lips and pushed down on the top, breathing in the bitter potion as the puff was released into her mouth. She held her breath for fifteen seconds - five longer than Will had recommended, for good measure - and repeated the process before stowing it in her pocket again. The sign went dark, and the big exit button filled with light.

Bridget reached out, and pushed the red button.

Immediately, the room began to fill with water. It was at her knees before she could react, but she realized she wasn't feeling the cold and her shoes didn't feel soggy. The waterproof charm was working.

She instinctively held her breath and closed her eyes as the water covered her lips, even though logically she knew the potion should be in effect.

Bridget waited a moment for the anxiety to settle in her stomach. Then she opened her mouth and took a deep breath. It felt just like breathing air. She opened her eyes. She could see perfectly clearly.

The room finished filling, and the front door opened.

Bridget stepped onto sand. Despite the waterproofing clip, she sank a little. She waddled forward until she was standing in the growing group of students surrounding Mr. Jerson.

"I know it's a bit disorienting," the teacher said. Bridget could hear him normally, despite being underwater. "You'll get used to it."

Gertie followed quickly after Bridget, grabbing her wrist as she pitched forward, not used to walking on wet sand. The waterproofing clip made it a lot easier, but there was still more resistance than walking through air.

Soon the entire club was in place, and turned to wait for Will to emerge from the entrance chambers.

When the door opened, to their shock, their tour guide swam out of the entrance chamber.

"One thing I should mention," he said as his tail hovered just above the sand. "I'm a citizen of Daallu. I use an Anthroform transformation potion and a work visa for Crescyth in order to act as a tour guide."

His shirt was still the same - a white button-up that seemed to be staying dry despite his lack of a waterproofing clip. He must have removed his pants in the entrance chamber, as his legs had fused into a green tail, seeming like a cross between a dolphin's and an eel's. Webbing had appeared between his fingers, its color a mix of his tail and olive skin. His green hair now matched the rest of his color scheme, and it floated back and forth in the water.

"We're a bit behind on our schedule," Will explained, swimming to the front of the group. "So you're going to have to ask me any questions as we go. Come along!"

They walked along a path made apparent mainly by the presence of tall, unlit lampposts on either side of them. Small strings of lights wrapped between the posts, giving the appearance of natural sunlight.

"At night, the lampposts come on and the star lights go out," Will explained. "Though letting outsiders come into the cities is a more modern practice, Mermaids have always ventured onto land. Many of the transformation potions that are used for a variety of purposes across the globe have their roots in Mermaid use. Anything that land dwellers had that Mermaids found interesting eventually developed a place down here, including light bulbs."

Gertie and Bridget gasped as they entered the outskirts of the city. Immediately, the land went from empty sand plains to a bustling hub. The star lights were no longer solely on lampposts, but strung between buildings, crisscrossing upwards and resembling starlit clotheslines. Mermaids swam above the club in great layers and numbers; almost no one was down at their level. The rounded buildings had doors on seemingly every level, allowing entrance no matter how far above the sea floor one was.

Fish swam alongside the Mermaids, in and out of buildings, apparently as ignored as a fly or pigeon would be.

"All right, gather around," Will said, stopping in the middle of what appeared to be a city square. The sand had become cobblestone under the group's feet, and it was a lot easier to walk. "That direction is the festival mentioned on the scavenger hunt." Will pointed in one direction. "That direction is the downtown district, where things like the library and museums are."

Mr. Jerson glanced at his watch. "It looks like we have two hours before our scheduled lunch."

Will clapped his hands together emphatically. "Right. I'll be leading a tour of the Great Daallu library, but if you want to skip that, feel free to go have fun and experience what Daallu has to offer. We'll meet at the tower two buildings that way at twelve o'clock sharp." He pointed at a blue spiral that stood above the other round buildings. "After lunch I'll take you on our scheduled tour of city hall and Daallu landmarks. That one is mandatory."

The groups of students who chose to participate in the

scavenger hunt ran off, but Bridget stayed near Will for a moment.

She read off of the scavenger hunt sheet, "What's one of your favorite locations in Daallu?"

Will grinned."Whirltown. It's a theme park with the best rollercoasters."

Bridget wrote down the answer with the waterproof pen Mr. Jerson had handed out. "Thanks!"

Gertie, Ernest, and Vivien were already huddled together, making plans.

"Okay, Ernest and I will go to the downtown district," Vivien was saying. When Bridget raised her eyebrows, Vivien explained, "There are questions about the orchestra house and art museums. They're our specialties!"

Bridget nodded.

"Then we'll take the festival and try to find these parks." Gertie pointed.

"And we can all try asking the questions of people who live here," Bridget said. "I got Will's favorite location so we don't have to ask anyone else that one."

"They have roller coasters?" Ernest asked, upon reading Bridget's sheet. "Nice!"

Gertie and Bridget moved through the city on foot, taking in the statues, the Merpeople, and the submarine-like vehicles that whirred above their heads.

"License plates are yellow and black," Gertie wrote on her sheet, upon getting too close to a vehicle.

Even the food was different. It seemed to be mostly raw fish, and the girls suddenly worried about lunch.

The festival that the scavenger hunt sheet mentioned was spread across the sand plains just outside the city. Large, colorful tents had been pitched, each promising great food, fun entertainment, or souvenirs. Bridget pulled Gertie away from a stall with hats, reminding her she didn't have any money anyway.

There were street performers with puppets and trained fish, child Mermaids swimming with their families, and music playing all around. The best part about the festival was that, since the tents were pitched on the ground, everyone was at their level down on the seafloor.

It was getting close to when Gertie and Bridget would have to leave and meet up for lunch, and they had filled out a good third of the scavenger hunt sheet, but no one knew the answer to the question they had come to ask.

"Hello," Gertie asked a Merman tending one of the stands that sold food. "Which mayor founded this festival?"

The Merman grunted and shrugged and continued helping a customer.

"Excuse me, ladies," a Mermaid swam up to Gertie, making direct eye contact so the human couldn't act like she hadn't heard. She was the only Mermaid they had heard speaking their language other than Will. "Would you like to buy some souvenirs?"

"No, thank you," Bridget said, knowing Gertie would want to buy everything and they didn't have a way to pay. She started to walk away, but Gertie didn't move an inch.

Bridget glanced at the Mermaid, and was shocked to see that her irises appeared to be an unnatural purple. Bridget felt compelled to follow her, even without eye contact.

It was her enchanted left eye that kept her from completely falling victim to the charm. With it, she could see things that couldn't normally be seen - enchantments, visions of the future, ghosts and the like. And it could see the spell radiating from the Mermaid's eyes, all of its energy focused on Gertie.

"We have some of the best deals on wares," the Mermaid continued, a picture of the ever-persistent saleswoman.

"Yes, thank you," Gertie said eagerly, walking into the tent the Mermaid pointed towards.

"Gertie!" Bridget followed her sister.

"What?" Gertie asked. "I want to see what they have!"

"We-" They walked into the tent, cut off from the electric light of the outside, and were shocked by what they saw.

They had been inside other tents in the festival - ones with food, acrobats, or books. They were all filled to the brim, trying to cram as much as they could into their allotted space.

This one was empty.

Gertie finally seemed to realize something was wrong as the Mermaid's spell wore off.

"What's going on?" she asked.

There was a noise behind them and they turned. The tent's flap had been pulled closed, and now three Mermaids, including the enchantress who had lured Gertie inside, were blocking their exit.

One of them had a gun.

"Hand over your money, tourists," the gunman said. "And we'll let you go."

Gertie stared in shock at the gun. Could it even shoot underwater?

Bridget inhaled sharply, upon seeing the layers of enchantments on the weapon that allowed it to work in the sea. Gertie took her reaction to be a very bad sign.

"We don't have any money," Bridget said. Gertie nodded, and reached for her pocket. The gunman's arm jerked to point the gun at her and she froze.

"I'm taking out my wallet," Gertie said, trying to keep her voice even instead of shaking in fright.

The gunman nodded his permission.

Gertie pulled her billfold from her pocket and threw it to one of the other Mermaids. As soon as it left her hand, it lost the effect of the waterproofing spell and became soggy.

The enchantress caught the wallet and pulled out the soaking dollar bills that were worthless in the sea.

"What do you have?" the gunman turned the gun on Bridget.

She put her hands up, and tried to tell them that she had left her entire bag, including her wallet, in the entrance chambers. But instead, she coughed orange.

Gertie's eyes went wide. "Bridget, the potion!"

Bridget coughed again, a cloud forming in front of her mouth.

"What's going on?" the gunman said. "What are you keeping from us?"

"It's just-!" Gertie started to shout, but then Bridget held up the orange inhaler as explanation.

"Is that a weapon?" the other Merman exclaimed frantically,

reaching into his jacket.

The gunman pointed the gun purposefully at Bridget, panic and anger in his eyes.

But before he could squeeze the trigger, the Merman yelped and dropped the weapon. As it slowly fell to the ground, the metal took on a warm yellow color. By the time it landed in the sand, it wasn't a gun anymore. It had been transformed into a banana.

The gunman fell forward, almost hitting the girls, as Peter Nessing tackled him. He'd used a speed spell to run through the tent flap and attack the mugger.

Gertie turned toward the other Merman, who had pulled out a knife and was heading towards her. She took a deep breath, and thought of the only spell that would help in this situation. The one she used to make ice with only a mini fridge in her dorm room.

"Freeze now," she said in the magical language of Laux. She held her hands out, shooting the magic from her palms. The spell froze the seawater in a line as it whirled towards the Merman. It wrapped him up with ice, until all that was moving was his eyeballs.

The enchantress swam out of the way of the spell, looped through the tent and began to summon a hex in her hands.

Bridget sprayed the second hit of the inhaler into her mouth, and, while holding her breath, jumped up to grab one of the horizontal poles that served as the skeleton of the tent. She swung and kicked the Mermaid as she came around, sending her into the fabric wall that bounced her to the ground.

As Peter held his target in a headlock, causing him to pass out from lack of oxygen, Bridget walked over to the enchantress, looking for something to restrain her.

A vision flashed before her eye; the Mermaid had a knife.

Just as the Mermaid reached up to stab Bridget, she jerked out of the way and caught the hand the blade was in.

"Nice try," Bridget snarled. She stood on the Mermaid's tail and twisted her arm until the knife fell to the ground.

Charlie Nessing walked in from the opening of the tent, where he had stayed after rendering the gun useless. He cast a spell that lit the sand under the enchantress blue. It began to shift, and though she struggled, the Mermaid sunk right into it. Bridget jerked back from the heat of the transformation, now understanding why the Merman had dropped his gun.

Charlie finished the incantation and the heat dissipated. The Mermaid struggled, but remained stuck in the sand. She snarled, and began shouting at the students in Mmeerruuk.

Gertie ignored her and went to Bridget, putting her hand on her sister's shoulder. "Are you alright?"

Bridget nodded warily, the familiar fatigue of seeing a vision taking its toll despite her adrenaline rush.

Charlie, as well, was worse for the wear. He panted from the effort of his spell and let himself collapse onto the sea floor, taking deep breaths.

Gertie kneeled in front of him. "Thank you so much for helping us."

"Please. Like we were going to let you get shot." Charlie rolled his eyes. "What were you thinking, looking straight into a transfixion enchantment? You'd be dead if we hadn't seen you."

Gertie shook her head. Even when saving their lives, Charlie had to be a jerk. She just said, "Thank you," right as the tent flap burst open, revealing three uniformed Mermaid police officers, ready to cast incapacitating magic.

"Freeze!" one shouted.

Charlie, Peter, Gertie and Bridget all raised their hands in surrender.

Gertie struggled not to giggle at how one of the Mermen was already quite frozen. The relief was getting to her.

The police swam in, Faye Nessing behind them.

"Oh thank goodness you're okay." She ran up to Peter and threw her arms around him. "Mom and Dad would have killed me!"

The police placed handcuffs on the unconscious gunman. After studying Charlie's handiwork, one of the officers threw her hands to the ground with a spell, and the Mermaid Charlie had sunk was uncovered, only to be immediately taken into custody.

The policeman stroked his chin as he studied the Merman Gertie had frozen.

"Is he alive?" he finally asked.

Gertie nodded. With the last remaining power she had, she cast the spell that would release the Merman, the one she used to thaw frozen meat before cooking at home. The ice cracked and melted, leaving the Merman shivering, but alive. He too was cuffed and led out of the tent.

It was then that Will and Mr. Jerson burst into the tent. Their eyes were wild, and they only started to relax when they took in everyone's calm posture.

"Is everyone okay?" Will asked.

The students nodded.

"How'd you know where we were?" Faye asked.

"Magic bubble," Will said offhandedly, pulling aside one of the police officers to speak to him.

The last officer wrote down the students' statements and took pictures of the scene of the crime. "Surely you know you should be more careful in cities," she said to them.

Bridget glared at her. "Surely you're not saying it's our fault that we almost got mugged."

"Come on," Mr. Jerson said, gesturing the students away from the tent. He didn't want the Mermaid officers to start pointing fingers at humans. "Let's get back to the meet up spot. It's time for lunch."

"One second," Gertie turned to the police officers, and whispered so the Nessings couldn't hear. "Do you happen to know which mayor established this festival?"

Gertie and Bridget go to a yard sale

"Ten dollars," Bridget said, countering the man's offer.

He sighed. "Fine, take the jacket."

Bridget pulled the bill out of her wallet and handed it to the man. She slipped the Fairweather jacket over her shoulders, smiling as it magically lengthened and grew to fit her, since its previous owner had clearly been much more petite. The material reacted to the sunlight, making the gray shimmer in blues and greens. It was quite the find, after digging through the large boxes of clothes where everything was marked as "name your price." Bridget loved going to yard sales.

Gertie looked through the potted plants sitting on a plastic folding table. She shifted aside the vines and leaves in search of stickers denoting prices, only to find the names of the plants instead. Her mouth popped open in a gasp, and she picked up one of the plastic pots.

"Is this a milkberry vine?" she asked the man running the sale.

"I don't know." He glanced over it. "I'll give it to you for three dollars though, since it's so tiny."

Gertie looked dumbstruck. "Don't you... but it's a milkberry vine!"

"My family tasked me with selling what they wanted to get rid of," the man said, typing numbers into a cash register and putting Bridget's bill in. "If they didn't put a price on it, or mention one to me, it's on them."

That was good enough for Gertie. "Sure. Three dollars."

She passed the pot to her sister and pulled out her new wallet to pay.

Bridget staggered under the weight - the plant was much heavier than it looked. It was barely more than a thick central stem with a few small black and purple flowers. The man was right; it didn't look like it was worth much.

"Can we go home?" Gertie said, excitedly taking the pot back from her sister.

"Yeah, let's-"

"Wait," the man stopped them. "You seem interested in magical things. All the furniture's been sold, and I can donate the clothes, but these are all useless to me. You want them?"

He held out a cardboard box. It contained several small boxes, some jewelry, a few books, and other random items. One thing was clear, through Bridget's enchanted eye that let her see such things: every item was somewhat magic.

"How much?" Bridget asked hesitantly.

The man sighed. "Fifteen for the whole box?"

"Deal!" Gertie said, putting down her new plant and pulling

out her wallet again.

❖ ❖ ❖

Gertie portioned out the water from a bottle into a drinking cup, meticulously measuring it down to the drop with a pipet.

Ziggy, the sisters' ghost dog, sat in front of her, begging her with soft eyes to play with him. Gertie almost wished she wasn't wearing her enchanted baseball cap that was spelled to let her see the ghost.

"Hey boy." Gertie reached down and attempted to pet him. Her hand went right through his fur, as he was incorporeal, but his mouth hung open in joy just the same. "I can't play now. I have work to do!"

"Come on, Ziggy. You can help me," Bridget said. He obediently lay down in the center of the room, next to Bridget who was still sorting through the box from the yard sale.

"What's so special about the plant anyway?" Bridget asked as she inspected a bottle.

"Milkberries are used in a lot of healing potions," Gertie said. She went to her bookshelf and got out the plastic container labeled "plant food." It was filled with a white powder that looked like baking soda. Gertie used it to enrich the soil and keep her plants healthy in her dorm room.

"So you want to learn healing potions?" Bridget asked, trying to figure out why Gertie was so worked up

"No. Well, yes." Gertie used the scoop inside the plastic container to measure out the plant food and mixed it into the cup of water. "But the berries themselves have healing properties, almost like their juice is a potion. I just figure that if we had an endless supply of fresh-from-the-vine healing berries, we won't have to keep going to the infirmary for bruises and scrapes."

"Wow!"

The tone was much too excited for what Gertie had said, so she looked up and saw her sister levitating.

Apparently, there had been an enchanted sunhat in the box that Gertie hadn't noticed. It now sat proudly on Bridget's head, allowing her to float.

"Mine!" Gertie said, running to her younger sister and trying to yank the hat off. Of course, Bridget was taller than her, and now she wasn't even on the ground. Gertie tried jumping, but couldn't get close to the hat.

"Why?" Bridget floated around the room, using her legs to paddle through the air, her feet just barely hovering, like Ziggy's were.

"I collect hats! I paid for the box."

"I don't know," Bridget said playfully and swooped to the side as Gertie grabbed at her. "I kind of like this. Maybe I'll start my own hat collection!"

Gertie groaned in frustration and threw the almost-empty water bottle in her hand at her dodging sister.

To their shock, the bottle hit Bridget's new jacket and, with a flash of light from the material, sprung away. It *whooshed* past Gertie's shoulder and crackled against the dorm wall, leaving a scratch in the paint. Ziggy yipped at the noise.

"Huh," Bridget said, removing the hat and thumping to the floor with both feet. She held the hat out to her sister, who took it with a quiet word of thanks. "Did the jacket do that?"

"Yeah," Gertie said. She placed her new sunhat on her desk to be stored later.

Bridget ran her hand over the fabric on her arm, watching the colors change and trying to discern with her eye what enchantments it had woven into it.

After a moment of thought, Gertie took a deep breath and took a fighter's stance with her fists up, facing her sister.

Bridget threw up her arms defensively. "What are you doing?"

"I'm going to punch the jacket."

"Why?"

"To test it."

Ziggy whined in protest.

"What if it reflects that badly back on you?" Bridget asked.

Gertie had already thought of that. "Then I get punished for trying to punch you."

"What if you actually hurt me?"

Gertie paused. "Do you have any other ideas?"

Bridget thought for a moment and shook her head, putting down her arms and turning to expose more of the jacket.

"Ok." Gertie pulled her fist back, and punched Bridget's arm.

The fabric her fist landed on lit up and felt like she had hit a wall instead of a person.

"Agh," Gertie shook her hand out, trying to relieve the pain.

"See!" Bridget grabbed a cold pack from Gertie's mini-fridge. "I told you it would hurt."

"Still," Gertie took the cold pack gratefully and put it on her bruised knuckles. "That's a useful jacket to have. I can think of a lot of fights it would have helped in. Did you feel anything?"

"No, nothing," Bridget murmured, her mind wandering to the possibilities.

Gertie looked to the box, full of unknown potential. "I wonder what else is in there."

The sisters sorted through the box, digging past the top layer they had seen at the yard sale. They found necklaces that stored power, a baseball that Ziggy could play with despite being a ghost, and old books on charm studies, magical creatures, and crockpot recipes. There were bottles and glasses, rags and soaps, a vase, a statue, and more. In short, an endless supply of weird things to test.

"What's going on?" Ernest came into the room without knocking on the open door, a beanie on his head.

"Look at all this cool stuff!" Gertie said, holding up an empty picture frame in front of her face. She pressed a button on the side, and the image of her expression froze as a painting in the frame.

"Nice." Ernest hesitated. "So, about that thing we texted about?"

"Oh, right!" Gertie sat up and went to her cupboard. She pulled a bottle out labeled with a "G".

"What's that?" Bridget asked.

"None of your business," Ernest snapped.

Gertie grabbed a second styrofoam cup from her stack.

Bridget stared at him. "It's a little warm for a hat, isn't it?"

It was Gertie who answered her. "It's *never* too warm for a hat." She pulled out some teaspoons and measured the potion from the bottle into the cup.

"I'm just saying." Bridget inched closer to Ernest. "Maybe something *else* is amiss?" She playfully reached for the tip of the beanie and Ernest backed away.

"Don't you dare!"

"Did the figgle get out of its cage and eat some of your hair?" she asked. The little pest had bothered Gertie for long enough before they caught it and Ernest offered to care for it. And its most common source of food was human hair.

Ernest turned beet red. "No!"

"Did it get out and eat *all* of it?"

Ernest balled his hands into fists. "Don't you dare laugh or I'll let it free into *your* room!"

Bridget bit her bottom lip, struggling not to giggle.

It was Gertie who did her in. "Ok." She set the cup down on the table towards Ernest. "I measured this perfectly so you don't accidentally grow hair on your elbow or-"

Bridget started laughing so hard she teared up.

"Oh screw you!" Ernest shouted, marching out of the room.

"Ernest, wait! I'm sorry!" Bridget chased after him.

Gertie sighed. She could hear them arguing in the middle of the hall. They would cool off soon enough. She packed away all their new magic paraphernalia that they had strewn over the floor and moved the box to a corner of the room where it would be out of the way. She took the cup, watered the milkberry plant, and fixed the angle of her growing light.

After still hearing the arguing, she sat on her bed, playing a game on her phone and petting Ziggy. A door slammed and then there was silence.

After a bit of waiting, she stopped to listen at her door. There weren't even footsteps.

Without warning, her door opened, nearly hitting her head.

"Everything good?" Gertie asked the no-longer-shouting Bridget and Ernest.

"Bridget's going to pay for dinner as an apology," Ernest said.

Bridget nodded. "You can come too."

"Great!" Gertie grabbed a light jacket off her computer chair.

"Gertie?" Ernest stopped her. "My potion?"

"Right." Gertie picked up the cup she had set aside and handed it to him.

"Gertie?"

"Yeah?"

"Is it supposed to be green?"

Gertie paused. She took the cup back from him. She smelled it.

"Nope, that's the plant food," she mumbled. She looked at the plant. It didn't look any different. But she had definitely just watered it with growth formula.

"Maybe it'll be fine?" Bridget said.

Gertie inspected the plant. It hadn't immediately grown to the ceiling of her dorm; in fact, it hadn't seemed to react at all.

Maybe this would be a good thing. Maybe the milkberries would grow faster.

Gertie shrugged, trying to shove that exciting thought down. "Well, nothing I can do about it now." She turned to Ernest. "Want me to make you another potion?"

Ernest waved his hand dismissively. "I'm too hungry. After dinner?"

※ ※ ※

Even before she turned on her light, Gertie knew something was amiss. Her room just didn't normally smell that sickeningly sweet.

She reached for the switch hesitantly, steeling herself for the worst.

"Oh," Ernest said, bumping into Gertie when she didn't walk farther into the room.

"Well, it looks healthier now," Gertie said.

The milkberry vine was no longer solitary. It had spread tendrils from its spot on Gertie's window sill, down the wall and up her bookshelf. It had almost reached her bed.

"Hopefully that's the worst of it," Gertie said. She picked up her pruning shears next to her plant pots, shaking a few leaves off of them, and began clipping away the flowerless vines.

"So." Ernest shifted awkwardly. "I guess I'm not getting the growth potion after all?"

Gertie shook her head. She had to deal with the plant. "Is tomorrow ok?"

Ernest nodded and left his hallmate to her task. Gertie spent the better part of an hour cleaning up the fallen tendrils and leaves, but by the end of the night she had her little milkberry vine back.

She changed, turned out the light, got in bed, and settled in to fall asleep.

※ ※ ※

When Gertie woke up, she found she'd been mummified.

It was a bit like opening up her eyes to find her worst nightmare had come to life. She fought against the urge to scream, and tried to sit up.

It took a bit of struggling, but the tangled vines that had grown over her in the night shifted aside, and Gertie took a deep breath.

The plant looked like it had exploded. Every place she had clipped a tendril, two more, thicker, longer ones had taken its place. Half her room looked like the corner of a greenhouse now.

Gertie grumbled. It was far too early for this.

She went to her computer, brushing off more plant matter, and started researching milkberry vine care.

"I brought you some - what the-?" Bridget stopped at the door, rendered speechless by the sight.

"Yeah, so," Gertie said, still staring at the computer. "It turns out that milkberry vines are notoriously hard to take care of. If you cut it wrong, or cut off any of its tendrils, it just grows another shoot. And the tendrils are useless - only the center vine grows flowers and berries."

Bridget moved closer to Gertie, setting down the to-go cup of tea she had brought her.

"Thanks," Gertie said and took a long gulp.

Ziggy, leaving Bridget's side, sniffed at the plant, trying to figure out what it was doing and how it got there.

"I apparently need to get some Cautopiary potion to brush on after I cut the smaller vines," Gertie said. "Otherwise this'll just happen again."

"Well," Bridget said. "Let's go get some then."

❊ ❊ ❊

"Wow, look at this." Vivien stepped into Gertie's dorm room gingerly, her west-Crescyth accent hard to mistake. "It's almost impressive."

"You're not helping," Ernest said. He had removed his beanie from the heat of the physical labor involved in bending and clipping off vines and brushing on potion for hours, and they could now see what looked like a five o'clock shadow on his head.

"Sorry," Vivien said. "How can I be of assistance?"

"Take this." Bridget handed her a garbage bag full of vines and leaves. "And walk it down to the dumpster."

The vine had lost most of its tendrils, and there was no sign of them coming back, thanks to the potion.

"Hey!" Gertie pulled a white berry from underneath some leaves, holding it up triumphantly. "Our first milkberry!"

"Nice!" Vivien said. Bridget and Ernest exchanged a look of frustration and got back to work. How could Gertie be so excited when they still had so much to do?

Gertie held the berry like a treasure. "I'm going to save this one-"

"Ouch!" Ernest held up his finger, a large gash in the side from where he had accidentally clipped it.

It was bleeding.

Gertie sighed. "Here." She handed over the milkberry. "Eat it."

Ernest looked at her hesitantly, took the milkberry and popped it into his mouth, chewed, and swallowed. He held his finger up again.

The four students watched as the cut slowly stitched itself together, leaving nothing but a drop of blood to signal that anything had been wrong in the first place.

"Well, that was-" Ernest paused and frowned. He reached up

and started scratching at his head.

Before long, his fingers were getting tangled in hair. His own hair.

"...Awesome."

With the last of the milkberry's powers, Ernest's hair had returned to its normal length.

"Well," Bridget said. "Looks like you got your growth potion after all."

Gertie and Bridget go to graduation

"Okay, sign the card and we're all ready to go!" Vivien said, capping the marker she'd been using.

It was graduation day at Flories Boarding School. Usually, Gertie and Bridget Mallon had nothing to do with such an event, but this year they'd made a group of friends, and one of them was graduating.

"I hope Ernest is excited," Gertie said, smoothing out the dress slacks she wore.

"Of course he is," Bridget said. She grabbed a pen and signed the bottom of the card Vivien had made. There was a drawing of the four friends across the top, and Bridget smiled sadly. It wouldn't be the same without Ernest. She passed the card off to Gertie to sign.

"Card, check," Vivien said, slipping it into an envelope and sealing it.

"Present, check." Gertie had a wrapped box sitting on her desk with a good microphone for recording music in it.

"Jackets?" Bridget suggested, looking out Gertie's window at the overcast sky.

"Don't need one!" Gertie said, placing a pageboy hat on her head that would make her and her clothing waterproof.

Vivien, meanwhile, held up her umbrella.

Bridget sighed and grabbed her Fairweather jacket. The gray complimented the pastel pink of her dress nicely and the hood would be useful in the event of rain.

On their way to the football field where the graduation ceremony was being held, Bridget, Gertie and Vivien came across Faye and Peter Nessing, talking between themselves and looking quite concerned. Peter, as a soon-to-be graduate, was wearing his graduation gown and holding the tasseled flat cap in his hands.

"We need your help," Faye said, stopping right in front of Bridget, her hands on her hips.

The other three girls stopped abruptly.

"What? Why?" Bridget asked.

"Our parents couldn't make it to my graduation," Peter explained. "Charlie's...pissed."

"To put it lightly," Faye added wryly.

"It's not his graduation though," Vivien said, furrowing her brow.

"It's just another in a long line of disappointments from them. Of them putting the mayoral race ahead of us." Peter shook his head. "It's the last straw for Charlie. He's going to do something to punish them."

"Okay, so why do you need our help?" Gertie asked.

"He put an enchantment on our dorm door," Peter said. "I can't get in even with my key."

Gertie glanced to the ground guiltily, already guessing where this was heading.

"We know you sneak off of campus, even with the magical protections." Faye crossed her arms accusingly.

"Ernest told us," Peter said. "Lockpicking, disabling the charm on the gate…"

"You have to help us get in so we can convince Charlie not to do anything," Faye finished. "We're not going to let him ruin his life over our parents neglecting us like they always do."

Gertie and Bridget looked at each other, hesitant to get involved.

"Besides," Peter said, his expression getting darker. "You owe us. We saved your lives."

Bridget was the first to nod. "Which dorm are you in?"

❀ ❀ ❀

"How are you so well-prepared as to have enchanted lockpicks in your purse?" Vivien asked, her accent coming through even in a whisper.

Bridget shrugged. "You never know what you're going to need."

Gertie, kneeling in front of the door, turned the tension wrench and the lock clicked. The enchantment on the Nessing brothers' door came down with it.

Peter rushed into the room.

Gertie saw his shoulders fall and knew Charlie wasn't there.

"He knew we'd get in," Faye said, patting Peter's arm. "We'll find him and convince him to stop."

Bridget glanced over the room, her eyes drawn to the bottom of Charlie's desk drawers. Her left eye had been damaged in an accident many years ago, and now let her see things others couldn't see. Including the leftover effect of a drawer having been transformed into a solid pane of wood.

"Shouldn't there be a bottom drawer there?" Bridget asked, directing the rest of the group to Charlie's desk.

Peter knelt next to the desk and ran his hand over the wood. There were a few raised edges where Charlie's magic hadn't been perfect. Peter knocked against the space; a hollow sound came back.

He took a deep breath and drew his fist back. Muttering a spell for strength, he punched the wood. He left a dent, in both the wood and his hand. He ignored the apparent injury, and drew back for another punch. It broke through, revealing the inside of the desk drawer.

Still using his bare, fractured hand, Peter broke away the rest of the transformed compartment, the wood cutting into his palm, and pulled out a notebook.

"What's it say?" he asked, handing it up to Gertie, his hand hurting too much to read it. In the meantime, the charm on his necklace went to work healing up the damage to knuckles and palm. Bones clicked back into place and the skin stitched itself back together.

Gertie glanced at the most recent notes with Vivien reading over her shoulder. There was a drawing of a person, with notes about composition.

"They're unveiling the statue of Julia Flories at the graduation today, right?" Vivien asked, recognizing the various metals and welding notes Charlie had written.

"According to the email they sent out," Faye said, looking up from checking that Peter's hand had healed correctly. "Why?"

"It looks like Charlie's going to use it for...something." Gertie flipped through the notebook.

There were notes on spells and transformations.

"Oh!" Vivien said, grabbing the notebook from Gertie. "He's going to make a miniature!"

"Of the statue?" Gertie clarified.

Vivien nodded. "If he gets stuff that the statue's made of, he'll be able to make a doll version of it and use a Fantosh spell to control the real thing."

Bridget already had her phone out and was looking at the email on graduation. "They said they wanted the statue to have the 'spirit of the founder of the school.'" Bridget stopped reading aloud to roll her eyes. "So they included materials from buildings that were on campus when Flories founded it."

"Which buildings are they?" Gertie asked.

"It doesn't matter," Peter said, rubbing his healed hand. "We just have to get to Charlie before he's able to do any of this."

Faye pulled out her phone and dialed a number.

They heard a ringing. Peter reached back into the hole in the desk and pulled out Charlie's phone.

"Alright, I'm using the tracing spell app then," Faye said. The app pulled a map up, revealing where Charlie was on campus. He could have been heading to any number of buildings.

As they watched, Charlie's dot moved along the paths through the school and his destination became clear.

"The library," Bridget realized.

"Great," Gertie said, clapping her hands together. "Let's go stop him."

❀ ❀ ❀

The sound of the school band at graduation floated over from the field, just beyond Charlie's goal, the tallest and oldest building in the school.

The group burst through the doors of the library, all eyes searching for the errant Nessing among the bookshelves and what they could see of the multitude of balconies.

Gertie sighed in frustration. "Charlie Nessing!" she shouted, trying out a gambit. "We can see you!"

There was a crash of a book cart being overturned from the third floor, and the group saw Charlie's mop of unruly brown hair dashing along one of the balconies.

Peter, Gertie and Bridget started after him.

"Guard the door!" Bridget shouted back at Vivien and Faye.

Peter scaled the bookshelves and jumped when he reached the top to grab the bottom of the next floor's balcony and pull himself up. Bridget and Gertie headed for one of the magical platforms that would raise and lower at their command.

"Third floor!" Gertie shouted. The platform flew them upwards, and Charlie, heading for the very platform they were on, came to a halt when he saw who stood there.

He turned on a dime and started running through the maze of bookshelves, hotly pursued by the Mallon sisters. They were going to make him sit and listen to reason before he could do anything to ruin the school's special day.

"Leave me alone!" Charlie shouted, knocking a table into the aisle.

Bridget jumped on its top and leapt off, losing no time. Gertie edged around it, slowing considerably.

"Charlie, stop this!" Gertie shouted, nearly out of breath as she picked up her pace again. "You don't want to get expelled, do you?"

"I don't care!" Charlie pulled a thick dictionary off a table and threw it straight at Bridget.

Bridget stopped and put her arms up in an X. The book hit the sleeves of her Fairweather jacket, and, thanks to the magic stitched into the fabric, ricocheted off and hit the floor without injuring her.

"Good idea wearing that jacket!" Gertie shouted as she caught up. The Mallon sisters were closing in on Charlie, managing to follow him even as he tried to lose them by changing aisles.

Charlie turned and shouted a spell. Magic burst from his fingers and hit some chairs. They shifted under his transformation charm until they were gates, blocking the girls' path. Bridget jumped over, while Gertie took a hard right to find a different path to Charlie.

He swore and kept running until he reached the railing that blocked the edge of the balcony, and looked out over the first floor. Vivien and Faye were standing guard at the front doors.

"Charlie." Peter stood a ways down the balcony. "Come on. Graduation is starting. Let's just go together."

Charlie gripped the railing until his knuckles turned white.

"Please?" Peter begged.

Charlie shook his head. "Mom and Dad are going to be here. I'm going to make sure of it."

Peter started towards Charlie. The younger brother grabbed a hardcover off of a nearby shelf and backed away, opening the book and tearing pages out of it.

Bridget and Gertie made it out of the bookshelves behind Charlie, and ran to grab him.

Charlie shredded the pages into confetti and threw them into the air, shouting a spell as he did so.

The scraps of paper turned inside out and became a swarm of bees.

"Oh f-!" Bridget shouted, pulling the hood of her jacket up in an attempt to deflect the bees' stings. "Gertie! Do something!"

"Smoke!" Peter suggested. "It'll put them to sleep."

"I don't know a spell for smoke!" Gertie said, and yelped as she was stung in the arm.

Charlie used the distraction to run past the girls to a platform. He hopped on and, too quiet for anyone to hear, said his desired floor. The platform rose, and he disappeared over the wood of the next balcony.

"I see a lot of things to burn!" Bridget suggested.

"Right!" Gertie snapped her fingers, saying, "Flame," in a magical language as she did so. The spell she used to make s'mores lit a flame above her thumb. She looked around wildly and hesitated. "Wait, I can't burn a book!"

"Are you kidding me?" Bridget shouted, receiving a sting

above her knee.

Bridget dug through her bag and pulled out a wad of napkins. She shoved them over Gertie's flame, dropping them onto the ground when they burned down to her fingertips.

An alarm started blaring and lights on the walls flashed.

"What's happening?" Peter shouted.

The front doors slammed shut and locked. The bookshelves shifted menacingly until they surrounded the group on all four sides, blocking their escape.

"It's some sort of security system," Gertie realized.

Magical clouds formed above the three students. With a rumble of enchanted thunder, rain began to spill down on them and the swarm, dousing Gertie's flame and the burning napkins.

Luckily, the bees still had some aspects of the paper they had originally been. They grew wet and soggy, and fell to the ground. Soon, there was nothing but what looked like spitballs under the group's feet.

The rain subsided as it had put the flame out, but the bookshelves still locked them in, waiting for someone bearing a punishment.

"Ugh." Peter's gown and the dress shirt he wore underneath were soaked.

Bridget's jacket had deflected most of the rain, but her open toed shoes had left her feet cold and clammy.

"Told you I didn't need a jacket," Gertie said, the hat on her head keeping her bone dry.

"What's going on up there?"

Gertie jumped at the voice of the librarian from the first floor.

"We've got to get out of here and stop Charlie," Peter said. "I can't believe he wouldn't listen to me."

One of the many ghost librarians of the Flories school library passed through one of the bookshelves keeping them captive, a deep scowl on his face.

"How dare you?" he shouted. Only Bridget, as a consequence of her enchanted eye, could see and hear him. "Our poor library! You will be severely punished!" he wagged his finger at the students. "The police are already on their way!"

"It's not us," Bridget quickly said.

"Vivien!" Gertie shouted, oblivious to Bridget's conversation. "Some help?"

"On our way!" was the faint reply.

"Not you?" the librarian repeated after Bridget. "Then who did this?"

There was a shake in the ground that pitched all the mortals off balance. The ghost, hovering above the floor, looked around, his anger shifting to concern. "What was that?"

"The one who's really responsible," Bridget said. "Let us go. We'll stop him."

The statement was punctuated by the sound of screams coming from the sports field. Charlie's plan was already underway.

"I can't move the bookshelves!" Vivien's voice came from outside their confinement.

The ghost librarian reached out and pushed one of the shelves. It responded to his touch, swinging open like a door to reveal a shocked Vivien and Faye on the other side.

"That boy you were chasing, with the glasses, he's doing this?"

the librarian clarified.

Bridget nodded.

The librarian hesitated, then said, "He went to the twelfth floor."

"Thank you." Bridget gestured that everyone should follow, and they loaded onto a platform.

"Twelfth floor," Bridget said. The platform raced skyward.

❋ ❋ ❋

The twelfth floor didn't even look much like a library anymore. There were some shelves nailed into the walls, with a few sparse books, decorations, and spider webs.

As the platform became level with the floor, Charlie came into view. He stood at a large window that he had opened, letting the cool air into the musty space.

Standing in the palm of his hand was what looked like a little metal doll. His other hand was casting a constant spell on it, causing it to move around his palm. It ran in place, ducked, and slammed into objects that weren't present for the miniature, but that the real statue was dealing with.

Within view of the window was the sports field where graduation was being held. The music had stopped. The only noise was the chaos, the shouting, the sirens.

Bridget could see from her vantage point that the statue of Julia Flories had destroyed the temporary stage that had been set up, knocked over the folding chairs the graduates had been on, and was now making a valiant effort fighting off whatever magical skills the teachers were using to try to stop it, matching the miniature move for move.

"It's over," Charlie said, not even turning his head to acknowledge his siblings. "I can hear the sirens."

"It's not too late," Peter insisted. "You can stop this now. Everything can go back to normal."

"What normal? The normal where we're not allowed to live our lives?"

"Charlie, no one got hurt, right?" Faye said.

Charlie scowled, not taking his eyes off of the large statue he was controlling. He had it break through the net of the soccer goal as it ran from a powerful hex cast by the spellcasting teacher.

"Of course not," Charlie spat. "This isn't about hurting anyone else."

"Then it'll be okay. We can work it out," Faye pleaded.

"I don't want it to work out," he said, glowering down at the ceremony. "I want them to pay. I want them to be so scandalized by me that dad will have to drop out of the race for mayor. He'll come home, and everything will go back to how it was. When it was okay for us to use magic."

"Charlie-" Peter tried.

"No!" Charlie looked over, his eyes wild. "You don't understand. It's all I'm good at!"

"What, using magic to get the drop on non-practitioners?" Vivien asked. "Cheating, and sneaking around, and hurting people to get what you want?"

"Shut up!" Charlie shouted.

"No! It's not okay! You *shouldn't* be allowed to do that!" Vivien started forward, only to be held back by Peter's firm grip. She flung her words across the room instead. "You don't even know how bad it is! Don't you see that what you're doing is why people *hate* magic in this city? Why they see all of you -- all of *us* as cheaters at the best, and monsters at the worst!"

"I said *stop*!" Charlie clenched his teeth and bunched his hand, nearly cutting off the spell he was using to control the statue.

Tears started to run down Vivien's face. "It's people like *you*! You're why I can't even tell my parents what I want to do with my life! You're the reason-"

"Shut up!" Charlie turned, throwing a spell towards Vivien.

Bridget moved quickly, stepping in front of Vivien and turning to put her enchanted jacket in between them and the spell.

The magic bolt hit the Fairweather jacket and bounced back, shifting from the hit and landing square on Charlie's chest.

There was a bright light that hid most of the bone-shrinking and feather-growing of the transformation. And when it faded, in Charlie's place stood an ostrich.

❀ ❀ ❀

The police were waiting outside the large doors to the library by the time the Nessings came out with Gertie, Bridget and Vivien trailing behind.

"What have we got here?" one of the officers asked, looking down at Faye, Peter, and the large bird that was Charlie Nessing.

"Our brother was the one that disturbed the library and graduation," Faye said. "He tried to turn her," she pointed to Vivien, "into a blue bird, and the spell reflected and he accidentally turned himself into an ostrich."

The large bird shook out its feathers and made a strange squawking noise.

"He says if you're going to arrest him you have to call our parents," Faye added, playing with a ring on her finger that she had just enchanted to allow her to understand Charlie as an ostrich. It now sat alongside her other bracelets and pendants that let her communicate with animals.

"Let me get this straight," the officer said. "You're claiming that your brother did all this, and then conveniently, and illegally, changed himself into an animal that couldn't use magic?"

"It sounds crazy, but it's true," Peter said.

The officer stroked his beard. "Just to be safe, I think you're all going to have to-"

"Wait!" the living librarian ran out of the library. Bridget, but no one else, could see that the ghost librarian that had let them out of their confinement floated quickly behind her. "There's someone who can verify their story!"

The librarian handed her glasses, enchanted to allow the wearer to see and hear ghosts, to the officer, who slipped them on.

He jolted at the sight of the floating librarian, but quickly recovered and took out his notepad.

It was an odd sight. An ostrich, some kids with bee stings, and a police officer listening to thin air, but by the time the ghost's account of what happened was finished, the police were ready to believe the students.

"Peter! Faye!" The nicely dressed couple that Gertie and Bridget had seen with the Nessings when they had toured the school ran to the threshold of the library and threw their arms around their children. The Nessing parents had arrived.

Charlie honked, flapping his wings.

"Of course I texted them," Faye said.

"What were you thinking?" Mr. Nessing demanded, turning to look at his ostrich son with a scowl. "Do you know what could have happened?"

Charlie bristled and made a booming noise in his throat.

"He says he knew exactly what would happen," Faye said. "You'd be forced to drop out of the race and everything could go back to how it was."

Mr. Nessing's face softened at that.

"You've got to admit, dad, you both have been so much busier," Peter said. "And missing my graduation kind of sucked."

Charlie honked.

"He says he managed to get you here though," Faye translated. "So you couldn't have been that busy after all."

"Charlie," Mr. Nessing awkwardly reached for his son's feathery shoulder. "I am so sorry that we made you feel this way. We had no idea."

Charlie made a noise that sounded like a scoff in his ostrich throat.

"Shut up and just accept the apology," Faye said.

Mr. Nessing frowned, obviously pained. "We have a lot of work to do, but your mother and I are willing to do it if you are."

Charlie softened. He lowered his long neck and headbutted his father's shoulder affectionately.

"Now." Mrs. Nessing turned to the assembled officers. "I called our lawyer on the way over here. We will drive with our children in our car down to the police station, where we'll be joined by our legal representation." She turned to the ostrich. "I'm glad we brought the SUV, Charlie. You'll have to sit in the back. And duck your head for the trip." Charlie shook out his feathers, his version of a shrug. She turned back to the police. "Is that acceptable?"

"Gertie, Bridget, Vivien." A crowd of students had assembled around the chaos unfolding at the library, and Ernest now stepped forward. "Where were you? And what's going on?"

The girls looked over the Nessing family, now including an ostrich, the police, and the miniature of the statue that was being bagged as evidence.

"It's a long story," Bridget said with a sigh.

❊ ❊ ❊

One week later, the temporary stage had been replaced, the folded chairs were put back into position, and the holes in the field had been patched up. Gertie, Bridget and Vivien sat in the bleachers with Ernest's older brother, all cheering as Ernest accepted his diploma from Headmistress Clearwater.

Ernest returned to his place and the Headmistress asked the entire senior class to stand.

The Nessing family sat together in the first row, with their ostrich son sitting on the grass in front of them, trying to keep his long neck out of the way as his parents snapped photos of their eldest son. Charlie had been bailed out, with the understanding that he would remain in his ostrich form until his proper trial so that he couldn't perform any magic.

Not that it seemed to matter to the Nessings. Peter smiled as he caught sight of his entire family, looking like he had never been happier as he stood with his class.

"Congratulations students. You may now move your tassels from the right side to the left."

The entire student body and assembled guests cheered, flat caps were thrown in the air, and the school band struck up the Flories Boarding School anthem. The statue of Julia Flories, sitting at the very back of the bleachers after being moved using Charlie's miniature, looked over graduation. It had a serene smile on its face, as if the school founder was entirely pleased with how her school had turned out.

"You know," Gertie said, looking at her sister. "I think I actually can't wait to come back next year."

Suddenly, Bridget could hear barking. It got louder, and soon their ghost dog Ziggy ran through the bleachers and their occupants, leaving a chill in his path, until he was floating in front of the Mallon sisters.

"Ziggy?" Bridget said. "What's up boy? What's wrong?"

Ziggy pawed the air, yipped urgently, and started nodding towards the dorms.

Bridget smiled at the irony. "Come on, Gertie. Looks like we've got one more thing to do before we leave."

Thank you for reading

TALES OF
MUNDANE MAGIC
Volume Two

Keep going for the bonus story
The Nessing siblings get transferred

A note from the author

Hello there!

Thank you for reading *Tales of Mundane Magic: Volume Two*! I hope you enjoyed it. For an independent author, it means so much to have such wonderful, supportive readers like yourself.

As a part of my extra big thank you, I've included a bonus story exclusive to this edition of *Tales of Mundane Magic: Volume Two*. It's a different sort of tale, but just as much fun.

The following story takes place shortly before the stories you have just read. Therefore, Charlie, Faye, and Peter Nessing have not yet met Gertie and Bridget or had any of the experiences you just read about.

Enjoy!

The Nessing siblings get transferred

A yellow-tinted monocle fell onto the desk in front of Charlie Nessing. He looked up into the expectant eyes of his older brother.

"Want to explain this?" Peter asked.

Charlie felt his chest tighten, but strained to make his face appear neutral.

"It's a seeing glass," Charlie said, moving as if to go back to his homework.

Peter leaned over him, his voice dropping to a hiss. "It's for checking blood impurity, Charlie. It's for blood magic."

"I know what the symbols mean, Peter. You don't need-"

"It was in your backpack!"

Charlie was grateful his brother was at least keeping his voice low during whatever intervention this was turning out to be. His bedroom was close enough to his parents' offices that he was sure they would hear shouting.

"Peter, whatever you think you've discovered, just tell me." Charlie impressed himself with how blasé he sounded in the face of his dark secret coming to light.

Peter took a deep breath and sat down on Charlie's bed, opposite his desk.

"It's that Sorcery Club at school, isn't it?" he asked, and Charlie's stomach swooped. So he did know.

"Yes," Charlie said, checking his glasses for smudges and rubbing them with a cloth anyway. "It's very interesting, Peter. You should think about joining-"

"How could you even-?" Peter shouted, then flinched, remembering he needed to be quiet. "How could you even suggest that? Charlie, they barely escaped that summoning last semester. They destroyed a whole hunk of the parking lot."

"That was a misunderstanding, Peter."

"I don't think anyone misunderstands. They're working on some dark shit, and it's going to get you in trouble."

Charlie looked up as Peter bent over him. It would have been threatening if it was anyone other than his brother.

"I want to pursue this as a career, Pete," Charlie said, trying his best to be earnest. "They keep us from learning about it in all the classes, but someone has to investigate these sort of things. Like Mom and Dad do, in the lab."

"Did," Peter corrected him, once again taking his seat on the bed. "You know Dad's going to quit."

Charlie waved his hand dismissively, not willing to consider his father's departure. "He'll be back. He's not going to win the race to be mayor."

Peter shook his head. "Don't change the subject. Sorcery, Charlie."

Charlie huffed and stood, walking the short distance to sit next to his brother. "I'm not doing anything dangerous. I'm just trying to learn."

Peter searched his brother's face. Seeing his longing, he clapped a hand on Charlie's shoulder and sighed. "Okay."

❊ ❊ ❊

Unlike school sanctioned clubs, the Sorcery Club met at midnight. As it was hard to sneak out, they did so over video chat.

"I know what we're going to try next," Debbie Echin hissed, her face lit eerily by her computer screen. "There's this great ceremony to be done by the dark of the new moon. We won't need much, just a few things..."

The connection wasn't great, so she kept momentarily freezing as Charlie watched and listened. She outlined the components they would need, the best place to meet at school, and when the cameras would be enchanted.

"That sounds great!" Francis Stewart crowed.

"Will you stop all that noise!" came from Francis' feed and he froze, eyes wide, hoping his father didn't come to check on him.

"Where are we going to get a vivistatic transducer, though?" Stilton Grange asked. "You need special licensing for that."

"The school has one in the back room," Francis supplied, his voice quieter. "I've seen it when Mr. Ackbuer sends me to get ingredients."

"Great, how are we going to get that before tomorrow night without anyone finding out it was us?"

"Charlie," Debbie said, and Charlie saw himself jerk to attention in his video feed. "I bet Sparkslab has a vivistatic transducer."

"Uh," Charlie whispered, blood pounding in his ears. "Yeah. It definitely does. My dad works with it, actually."

"Perfect." Debbie's smile was wide, her braces reflecting her screen. "Can you get to it?"

What would Peter say to that if he found out?

Still, the ritual sounded fascinating. He could easily get whatever he needed from the lab, and it would be back before anyone noticed. Besides, Peter wasn't his boss.

"Definitely," Charlie promised.

❊ ❊ ❊

"Hi Dad."

Mr. Nessing swung around, his elbow almost hitting a cabinet from the way he held his phone up to his ear. He frowned and put one finger up for Charlie to wait.

"That sounds perfect," Mr. Nessing said. "Can the rest wait? Maybe ten minutes? Thank you."

He hung up and smiled down at Charlie. "What can I do for you?"

Charlie smiled hopefully. He, Peter and Faye used to spend tons of time in Sparkslab. His parents often showed them the experiments they were doing, or let them try new spells out themselves. The staff all knew him, which is how he was able to stroll in, even when his dad didn't know he was coming.

"I had some potions homework I thought would be easier to do here than at home," Charlie said. "Plus, it's been forever since I've seen any new witchery, and I thought you might have something interesting to teach me."

Mr. Nessing waved his hand. Charlie almost mistook it for a spell, and his heart sank when he realized it was a dismissal.

"I haven't had time for much. You can ask your mother; she's been working on a fascinating use case for possession."

Mrs. Nessing worked in a lab on the floor beneath her husband's. If Charlie wanted to talk to her, he could have. It would have been easier. But she didn't work with a vivistatic transducer. Even as he was listening to his father, Charlie could see the locked cabinet in the back of the lab with a cylinder of floating silver liquid sitting among other magical artifacts.

"Dad, can't you just show me what you *are* working on?" Charlie said, and he felt six years old, asking his dad to show him how a simple levitation spell worked. Back then, Mr. Nessing had fetched a stool and taught Charlie by hand how to raise a pencil into the air.

But Mr. Nessing's phone rang and he answered it.

"Yes, I know it's urgent," Mr. Nessing told the caller. To Charlie, he said, "Feel free to do whatever you need for homework. If you want help, your mother is downstairs."

Then he left the lab room, probably going to a quiet conference room nearby.

Charlie sighed, hefted his backpack up on his shoulder, and walked over to the locked cabinet.

There was no key, passcode, or scanner keeping the door to the ingredients locked. Instead, there was a small wooden panel between the door and the jamb with a needle next to it. A blood lock.

Charlie smirked. Clearly, there were real-world applications for sorcery.

Charlie pricked his finger and smeared blood on the wood. It soaked in, not leaving behind a trace.

Blood magic was perfect for keeping away strangers who wanted to steal something. Except when someone of your own bloodline came knocking.

The door to the cabinet opened. Charlie took the silver cylinder and tucked it in his backpack, which he had lined with a dampening spell that could fool systems meant to scan for these sort of things as he left the lab.

Charlie waved to the administrator as he left, clearing the detectors. *They really ought to improve their systems*, he thought. *It makes sense that school wouldn't, but a private laboratory?*

Just as he thought he was clear, Charlie recognized the car pulling up to the curb. Peter lowered the window.

"Get in," he said, his voice steely.

Charlie opened the back door and slipped inside.

Faye, Peter and Charlie's younger sister, sat with a cat in her lap. Charlie recognized it as one of kittens they had kept when their first cat gave birth, but couldn't distinguish it beyond that. The cats all slept in Faye's room.

"What did you do?" Peter asked as the magical autodriver took the car out of the parking lot and back towards the Nessing house.

Charlie's heart hammered in his chest. "I don't know what you mean."

"Tell me-" Peter rubbed his eyes. "Tell me you didn't just go into our *parents' lab* and...and steal-"

"How did you even know?" Charlie shot back. "Were you spying on me?"

"Killian was hunting for mice last night," Faye said. The cat purred in her lap. "He heard you. I was asking if anyone knew where you went after school and he told me you went to get that 'fur-fur-static tom-mouser' from the big ones' other house and-"

"Big ones? Other house?" Charlie repeated.

"Do not change the subject," Peter said. "What are you doing? Do you know how much trouble you could get into? How much trouble Dad could get into if the news found out?"

"I'll put the transducer back after!" Charlie said. "It's not going to get damaged. Everything is going to be fine."

Peter opened his mouth as the car pulled into their driveway.

"Don't you trust me?" Charlie interrupted Peter. He looked up into the rearview mirror, making eye contact with his brother.

"Not really," Faye said, and Peter laughed.

"Well, I do," Peter said. "Make sure you think this all through, Charlie."

Charlie nodded. "I have. Would you maybe mind dropping me off at school? The new moon rises early in the winter."

Faye snickered and Peter sighed, but told the auto driver to take them to Poincell Preparatory Academy.

As he looked in the rearview mirror, Peter noticed Charlie wriggling in his seat. That was probably for the best, if he was uncomfortable. Maybe he'd see the error of his ways on the short drive.

Faye was no help in convincing Charlie. She just scrolled on her phone, stroking the cat that was curled up on her lap.

Peter rolled his eyes at her and focused on his brother. Charlie stared out the window, his backpack with the borrowed vivistatic transducer sitting on his lap. He had to know that what he was doing was wrong, right?

When the car pulled up to the school drop off area, Charlie undid his seatbelt.

"See you later. I'll get home myself," he dismissed them, and ran onto campus.

Peter groaned and let his head rest against the steering wheel.

"We should stay, right?" Faye piped up.

"Yes, we should," Peter said, his voice muffled.

After a few minutes, Peter heard Faye murmur, "Hm…"

"What?"

"Did Charlie mention what they were going to do with the transducer?" Faye asked.

"No."

"Because I'm looking up 'vivistatic transducer' and 'new moon' and nothing good is coming up."

Peter jerked his head up. Faye actually looked nervous.

"What do you mean?" he asked.

"There's this ritual called the Binding Assimilation and it, uh, it involves taking a living thing and uhm…"

Peter didn't need more of an explanation if Faye was antsy. He tore out of the car, running blindly into the school after Charlie.

❈ ❈ ❈

"Great, you got it," Debbie said, reaching out for the vivistatic transducer that Charlie pulled out of his backpack. He peered down at her, frowning.

"What's with the alchemy circle and the rat?" he asked, pointing down at an enchanting circle that had been sketched on the ground with charcoal, and a black rat from one of the biology cages that had its paws tied.

Debbie waved her hand dismissively. "It's nothing."

"You said we were working on a transformation spell," Charlie said. "This looks more like-"

"Just give me!" Debbie snatched the vivistatic transducer from Charlie's hands and swung her other hand out at him, releasing sparks of fire as she slashed. Charlie instinctively raised a magical shield, backing away.

"It's going to be fine," Debbie said haughtily, smoothing her hair.

Charlie wasn't sure, but if there was one thing he knew, it was that no one got to talk to him like that. He dissipated his shield and crossed his arms.

"Maybe I should take back my father's property," Charlie said, trying to take on the menacing air of confidence Peter always seemed to exude.

"Careful Charlie," Debbie said, glaring at him. "How would your father react to knowing it was *you* who got the summoning circle wrong last semester? People could have died, you know."

Guilt flashed through Charlie's chest, followed closely by shame and acceptance. They all knew the wrongdoing of everyone else in the group. They were in this together.

The rat struggled as Debbie lowered the vivistatic transducer next to it. The silver liquid started sparking, responding to the power of the new moon rising.

Stilton looked sick to his stomach as Debbie began stoking the power of the circle by blowing magic on it. As if it were hot coals, the charcoal circle began to glow.

Francis knelt on one side, eyes locked on Debbie as she began to read out loud from a book of sorcery.

"Cavorey carveret roostep-stoo..."

Powered by Debbie and controlled by the vivistatic transducer, a great funnel of magic rose up from the circle. It roared like a barely contained fire, sparking red as it swirled and grew.

Charlie watched angrily as the rat stopped moving, but he was too cowed by Debbie's threat to do anything to save it.

The tip of the funnel touched Francis' chest, and his eyes rolled back into his skull.

Absorbing another creature's life energy was never pleasant, even if it was just a rat. Charlie could at least have satisfaction with that.

But then, in a last burst of stamina, the rat screamed and rolled just outside of the circle boundary.

Sparks started flying up from the charcoal circle and wind whipped up from the collapse of the spell. Charlie darted in front of Stilton, throwing up another energy shield as the sparks and wind set the wooden desks alight.

"Shit!" Debbie shouted, flipping through the book for a counter as the spell continued to pull energy from her.

Francis collapsed, his face pale as the funnel that had been gifting him life started to drain it.

The smell of ash and the burn of heat was forcing its way past Charlie's shield. His mind whirled. If the funnel grew to encompass him and Stilton, it would drain their power first, and then their lives.

The door to the classroom opened and Charlie looked up in surprise. It was Peter.

Charlie's older brother ran to him, ignoring the fire of the room with the experience of someone who felt pain often and was used to healing magic. He skirted around the funnel that swelled as it sought a new victim.

"We've got to contain it," Peter shouted over the noise of the spell. "A Sparkness circle could probably cut it off from both Debbie and Francis."

Charlie looked over to the two other club members. Debbie had fainted, and Francis was lifeless on the floor. He might already be dead.

"Right," Charlie quickly agreed. The swirling smoke was overpowering his senses, and it was all he could do to keep his energy shield up.

A spark hit Peter in the face and he hissed. When he wiped it away, there was a bloody hole in his cheek.

"Give me your hand," Peter said, holding out his own.

Keeping his other hand out to maintain the spell that protected him and Stilton, Charlie locked his grip with his brother's. The feeling of their magic joining was a familiar practice. They might as well have been trying to loot their parents' liquor cabinet.

Peter cast the spell, looping in Charlie's magical power as necessary. Charlie started to get tired, and struggled to stay conscious with all this expenditure.

Peter spoke the closing words of the containment enchantment, and a new circle glowed from the floor, like green electric tape glowing in the night. Beams of light shot up from the ground, cutting off the funnel from Debbie and Francis, its sources of power.

Slowly, as Charlie watched, the funnel began to dissipate like a cooling fire. It lowered to the tiles and vanished. The charcoal circle on the floor went cold, and all was quiet.

After a breath, Peter started casting spells to put out the desks and cool the flames on the walls. Stilton eventually joined in, embarrassed from being paralyzed by fear when there was actual danger.

"Thank you," Stilton mumbled to Charlie as he slowly lowered his shield.

Charlie ignored him and strode over to Debbie, and then Francis. They were severely weakened, but breathing.

"Check the rat," Peter ordered as he used telekinesis spells to clear a path to the door. "Faye will want to know." There was a crash as the spell shoved the desks and chairs aside.

Trying to hide his shaking, Charlie knelt next to the rat's still body. He snapped his fingers and cast a simple spell to release the bonds on its paws.

Immediately, the little rodent that had been playing dead leapt to its feet. It squealed and ran off through the path Peter had cleared to its freedom.

"Yeah, it's fine," Charlie grumbled. He looked down at the charcoal circle. The vivistatic transducer, and everything else

Debbie had used to cast the spell, had been destroyed. "Dad's going to kill me," Charlie groaned.

"Right, that's what's important right now," Peter said.

"I'm getting out of here," Stilton said, looking around the room. The entire place was covered in ash, and destruction was evident.

"They're going to know it was us," Charlie spat. "Even if Francis did disable the cameras, the teachers know which of us are in the club."

"I don't care," Stilton said, and ran from the room.

Charlie took an unsteady breath as he reviewed the situation. Debbie and Francis would need medical help, but if he called a hospital then they would know what they all did.

Peter bore down on Charlie. "Explain how we're going to keep all this mess from being connected to Dad."

It took Charlie a few seconds to realize what he was even saying. "I'm sorry?"

"You stole the transducer from Dad. He's trying to run on a platform of responsible magical use. Explain how we're going to keep this from demonstrating to the public that he is irresponsible with magic, to the point of letting his son get his hands on a dangerous magical artifact and nearly killing three people with it?"

"That's...This isn't *my* fault!"

"You think that's how the papers are going to see it?" Peter asked. "Dad's political career is dead."

Charlie fumed. "Well, maybe this is all for the best then! I don't even want him to be mayor!"

"And this is all about you, isn't it, Charlie?" Peter snapped.

Charlie felt his face go red hot with shame.

Peter took in his brother's expression and sighed. "Let's get out of here. We can get back to Faye and figure out what to do."

Charlie was silent as they walked back towards the parking lot where Peter had left the car. Peter fumed; this was the exact reason he didn't want his brother getting involved with dark magic.

Peter was surprised when there were two cars parked in the drop off area of the parking lot instead of just his. But then he recognized the second car.

"What is Dad doing here?" Charlie hissed.

Peter hung his head as they approached. Faye stood next to their father, holding the cat in one hand and a vivistatic transducer in the other.

"Where did that come from?" Charlie balked.

"I'm going to be doing the talking," Mr. Nessing said, his voice just on the restrained side of furious. "Here is what happened tonight. The other kids in your little club stole the vivistatic transducer from the school. Faye is not holding one right now, because mine is safely back in my personal cupboard at home, since I took it from work this afternoon. Charles, you had no idea what they were planning-"

"I didn't!" Charlie yelled and Mr. Nessing glared down at him.

"You had no idea what they were planning and were able to stop it due to your skill and training," Mr. Nessing continued. "I, of course, am horrified that the school would be vulnerable to its students performing such a dangerous ritual, which is why I'm pulling my children and my lab's funding from it."

"What?" Charlie shouted.

Mr. Nessing continued as if he hadn't heard him. "Peter, you and Faye are going to return home. Immediately."

Peter looked at Charlie, who glared at the ground.

"Charles, you're going to call the police," Mr. Nessing continued. "You called me first, because you were scared, but I told you we had to look out after your friends, even if they made unwise decisions. I arrived just before the police did."

Charlie didn't say anything, but took out his phone obediently.

Peter got in the driver's seat of his car and Faye got in the back.

"How did you get the vivistatic transducer from the school?" Peter asked.

"The cameras were off," Faye explained as the car pulled away from the school. "I mean, I can only assume they were for all the stuff the club was doing. I sent Killian in with an unlocking spell on his collar. He brought me back the transducer after I explained what it looked like."

"Did he drag it with his teeth?" Peter asked. The car headed for home.

Faye just shrugged in response.

"Did you call Dad?" Peter demanded.

Faye met his eyes using the rearview mirror. "I had to. He's going to fix it. Otherwise Charlie could go to jail."

Peter looked away from her to stare at the road. He thought of everything his father had said. They were going to leave Poincell Preparatory Academy. Where would they go? He was almost done with his last year. Things were supposed to be smooth sailing.

The two siblings arrived home without incident. Their mother looked down at them, lips pursed. She hadn't changed out of her work clothes, and still wore the crisp white lab coat with *Sparklabs* embroidered on the front.

"You knew what Charlie was doing," she said. It wasn't a question.

"You try to stop Charlie when he has his mind set on something," Faye chirped.

Mrs. Nessing shook her head, struggling not to smile. "I hear we'll need to find a new school for you."

"Good luck with that," Peter snapped, to his mother's surprise. "I'll be in my room."

An hour and a half later, Peter heard the front door open and close. There were low tones from his mother and father speaking at the base of the stairs. Then there was the sound of angry footsteps, and Peter's bedroom door burst open.

"Hey," Charlie said, throwing himself down on Peter's bed.

Peter gave a long-suffering sigh and turned away from his laptop and desk to face his brother. "How are you doing?" He knew his brother used up a lot of magical energy that night. On top of everything else, he must be exhausted.

"Great," Charlie said, but it was full of acid.

Peter felt bile rising in his throat. It was Charlie's fault they were in this mess. They *all* had to leave their school and friends behind, because of him. Peter opened his mouth to tell him so.

But then Charlie rolled away from him and hiccuped, and

Peter realized he was trying not to sob.

All the anger drained out of him.

"It's okay," Peter said, standing and walking over. He placed a hand on Charlie's shoulder, and watched silent tears drop down Charlie's face.

"I hate this," Charlie said, and sniffed. "Where are they going to send us?"

"I don't think they know," Peter said.

There was a quiet knock on Peter's door.

"Come in."

Faye stuck her head inside. "It's going to be okay," she said. "I have the perfect solution."

She placed her laptop in front of them, open to a school website.

Flories Boarding School, it read. *The number one rated public boarding school in Tornstead.*

"Great," Charlie groaned. "They'll send us away, where we can't do magic."

"Not so fast," Faye said. She clicked through to an FAQ page.

Does Flories teach magic?

True to Julia Flories' vision, we offer magical and non-magical classes side by side. If even one student wants to take a magical elective, we make room for it in the curriculum. Flories has a long history of magic; there's no better place to learn the secrets of our world.

Charlie stared at the screen. "Well, it's worth a shot."

Acknowledgements

My sister Devyn is one of the most incredible people in my life. It was on the phone with her that I first came up with the characters of Gertie, Bridget, and Ziggy, and we are constantly supporting each other's writing. She's taught me so much with her own skill as a playwright, and by being an amazing person.

My parents, Lee and Kathy, have supported me in everything creative I've ever done. I couldn't have accomplished any of this without them.

My partner, James, thinks as critically about my writing as I do, and I've never met anyone else that could read my full-length novel in a few days. I wouldn't write half as much as I do if the music he writes and plays wasn't so inspiring.

My friends Meg, Alex, Cheyenne, Steph, Britt, Deanna, Patrick, Aaron, Sahar, Ava, and loads of my coworkers have been so incredibly supportive of my writing, whether they've been reading for years or just offered advice on publishing *Volume One*.

About the author

Shaina Krevat's other job is a Software Engineer at YouTube, which is kind of her dream. She graduated from UC Berkeley with a BA in Computer Science, several best friends, and five full-length novels that she put on indefinite hiatus.

In her free time, she cooks, tries to teach her dog Atlas how to sit on command, posts writing advice, and wonders if she'll ever figure out how to get Link to walk in a straight line in *Breath of the Wild*.

She lives in Los Angeles with Atlas and her partner James, where they work on their respective creative endeavors and puzzles.

You can follow her @shainakrevat, visit her websites shainakrevat.com and talesofmundanemagic.com, and purchase her first book on Amazon.